Justice fo...

Nikki Mays

Nikki Mays

Published by Nikki Mays

Cover Design: Tracie Douglas @ Dark Water Covers

Photographer: Reggie Deanching @ RplusMphoto

Cover Model: Matt Mueller @ The Stable & Models of RplusMphoto

Editing: Golden Life Publishing

Formatting: T. L. Mason

Dedication

As usual, I would like to thank my husband for his unwavering support. Thank you so much for always being supportive about my writing. You have no idea how much I truly appreciate you.

I want to thank my mom for helping me so much all of the time! While writing this book, I had back surgery. My mother literally moved in with us for a few weeks so that she could take care of my children for me. I don't know what I would do without you Mom. I love you!

And just thank you to my amazing readers! Thank you so much for reading what I write! When I first started, I never thought that anyone would actually be interested in anything that I have to write. All of you have made my dream a reality, and I thank you for that.

Finally, I want to thank my editor Brooke for all of her hard work. She makes sure that all of my words are pretty, coherent and not redundant! I also appreciate the fact that you get so into the stories and really edit with my vision in mind. It's a great feeling to have someone at your back who gets what you want and tries to help you accomplish it.

Table of Contents

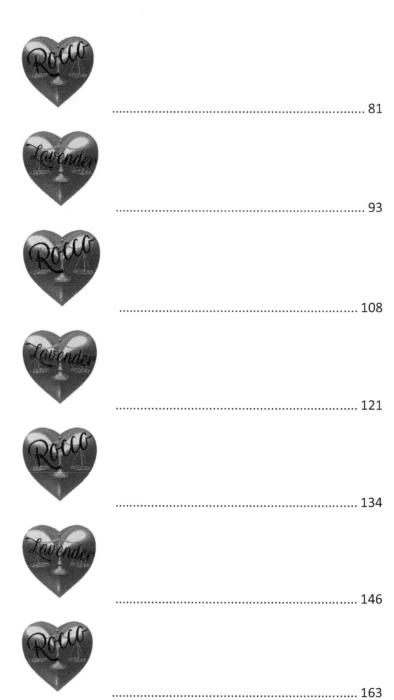

No, no, no this can't be happening! This has to be wrong! These tests are always wrong. I've heard of false positives. Yes! That's what this is. I'll just go back to the store and get a different brand and retake this and I'm sure that it will come back negative. It has to, I think to myself as I stare down at the test on the sink. I take a deep breath and look at my pasty reflection in the mirror.

There is no way that I can be pregnant by a man that I'm not even dating. A man that I try with all my might to stay far away from. Squeezing my eyes shut, my mind drifts back to that one time in Vegas. Stupid sister's wedding. Stupid tequila shots! I barely drink wine, how was I supposed to know that I would become a damn tramp and practically maul that man of my every dream and fantasy.

That's it! It's those darn dreams and the stupid tequila's fault. Plus, I'm not even one hundred percent sure that anything really happened. That whole night after Sage and JJ got married is pretty much just one big blur. And, okay, sure, I did wake up naked as a jaybird in Rocco's room. And sure, our clothes were thrown haphazardly all over the room.

Easing myself to the floor I can't help but think of waking up in bed with him wrapped around me like an octopus. I still remember the soreness between my legs. Maybe I got really drunk and thought that riding one of those mechanical bulls was a great idea. They have those things in like every bar...right?

So, yep, I totally did not have a one-night stand with the man of my dreams. I then did not slither out of bed carefully so as not to wake him. I definitely did not get dressed faster than a fire fighter going to a call. And I can assure you that I did not creep out of his room and back to my own praying that no one would see me. I also, did not make sure that I was nowhere near him for the rest of the trip.

All of this sounds completely legit. Right. I can do this. I am a well-educated, grown woman for Christ's sake. Any moment now, I am going to get off of my bathroom floor where I have been sitting for the last five minutes – possibly an hour- and I am going to drive myself to the store to get a different test. Easy peasy lemon squeezy. What? I may be well-educated but I still teach five-year-old's for a living....cut me some slack.

Any minute now, I will stop staring at this tiny test like it's a ticking time bomb. It's not like it's going to jump out and whack me in the face. And so what if I am pregnant? I'm an adult, with a stable job and health insurance. I can definitely raise a baby at my age. I mean, my sister Sage had twins at sixteen. If she can do that as a teenager, well then I can very well raise a wonderful child as a grown woman.

I jump sky high when my phone starts ringing on the floor next to me. My heart is hammering in my chest. I look at the caller id and see that it's the man that I've been studiously ignoring. I do have a sneaking suspicion that it was either my sister, Kayla or Declan who gave Rocco my number.

Now that Sage and Kay are ridiculously happy and in love, they think that everyone should be. I'm happy for them, but it does not mean that I need to be near the man that makes me too nervous to even form words. Declan, well, he's just a big busy body. I absolutely adore the man, but gosh can he get all up into your business. I swear that charming smile and those innocent little boy eyes are so hard to resist when he insists on being part of your life.

Not that I mind having him in my life. Thanks to him, I'm constantly laughing at something that he says or does. He really is a blast to be around. Except when he's being a busy body and trying to push me – ungently – into the arms of his friend. I actually have a sudden flash back of Declan doing just that in Vegas with a big cheesy smile on his face.

I swear, if he played any role in this – totally false positive – pregnancy, I'm going to kill him! Okay, I probably won't even yell at him but I will cry to Sage and Kay. They can be very mean when they want to be. It's one of the perks of having an awesome older sister. She deals with the people that I can't.

She's always been the outgoing, take no crap, in your face and I'll do whatever I want one. I'm always more of the one to stay quietly in the shadows. I tend to get a little tongue twisted in front of a lot of people. I can easily command an entire class of children but staff meetings make me want to dry heave...go figure.

I ignore the ringing. When it stops and starts again, I'm tempted to fling it off my lap. Why won't he just give up! I swear this man is the most stubborn and infuriating man in the entire world! Doesn't he understand that I can absolutely not function around him, well unless I'm drunk apparently. Why can't he just fixate on any of the gorgeous women that are constantly vying for his attention anytime that we've all been out together?

Why in the world would he want an overly average woman like me, when bombshells practically throw themselves at him? I just don't get it. And it's not like I think that I look horrible, because I don't, I know that. But dull brown hair, muddy brown eyes, lips too big for my face, a weird tiny nose and a weird pear-shaped body – Sage calls it hourglass – with medium sized boobs, does not even come close to being in the league of a man like Rocco.

Seriously, the man's body is a work of art. Luckily for me, Danny and Sage opened up a gym and all the guys like to work out there, especially Rocco. Have I mentioned that the Adonis is usually shirtless when he's working out? I've never liked going to a gym as much as I do these days. And I know for a fact that I'm not the only one who enjoys the show. Several other teachers have come with me after work to *"catch the show"* as they call it.

He's so tall, probably at least 6'3 and he is all muscle. Every inch of his body is like granite. Unlike the other guys, he doesn't have tattoos all over his body. He just has one arm completely covered and it looks amazing every time he flexes his muscles. He has dirty blonde hair and hazel eyes that change color with his moods...not that I've paid that much attention to that or anything.

Oh, who am I kidding, I am totally a stalker, except I try to stay away from him when he's actually near me. I probably suck as an actual stalker. But I swear that the minute he turns those hazel eyes in my direction, my usually over active brain goes entirely blank.

I can't even seem to form coherent syllables whenever he's near me. It's so embarrassing, especially since it's obvious that it's just him, since I can speak like an adult to every single other person in the darn world!

This will be an absolute disaster if I really am pregnant. Let's not even get into the fact that I didn't think that I would actually ever be able to have children. I'll have to co-parent with the man of my dreams, whom I can't say even simple things to when he's near me. Then there's going to be my heart getting completely crushed when he eventually finds a gorgeous woman whom he'll marry and have tons of other babies with. I feel like a Debbie Downer as my mind rambles on.

The phone starts ringing again and I finally can't take it. I answer the thing and kind of wish that I could take back that momentary lapse in judgment...well two of them if I'm being truthful.

"Hi, Rocco."

Finally! Finally this infuriating woman answers the damn phone! And damn does her voice saying my name send chills running down my spine and to other body parts.

"Hello, sweetheart." I say gently trying not to spook her. That seems to happen any time I even get near her. She's worse than a horse seeing a fucking snake. "How are you?"

I slap myself on the forehead. I finally get her to answer the phone and this is how I'm starting out? Not why did you skip out on what was the best night of my entire life...the parts I can remember anyway. Not why did you make sure that you were never anywhere near me ever again. Not why have you been ignoring every phone call, voicemail and text message that I've left you.

Okay, that sounds pretty stalkerish, but I swear I'm not completely stalking her. If I happen to be where she is – often – well then so be it, that just means it's fate. Okay, it means that I have great friends who are helping me stalk the woman of my fantasies and now vivid dreams. But hell, I just can't catch a break when it comes to her. She'll talk to everyone but me! Do you have any idea how frustrating it is to have the woman that you would do anything to get a simple date with, ignore your entire existence?

If I wasn't convinced that she was by far worth it and my end game, I swear that I would've fucking called it quits months ago. But after Vegas, that's not even in the realm of possibilities any longer. She's going to be all mine, even if I have to pull a Damon and stalk her fine ass for two years! I look up at my ceiling. Lord, please don't let it take years. I don't have the same will power that Damon does. He's a freakish bastard and trained sniper, I just don't have it in me.

I let my legs dangle over the edge of the couch, while sinking further into the cushions. Besides the silence on the other end of the phone, I could hear the sportscaster speaking from the T.V. in my kitchen. At the sound of her voice, I tune back in.

"Oh, umm, I'm, you know, *cough* I'm okay." She stutters out adorably. "How are about you? I mean how about you? How are you? That's what I meant to say."

I'm glad that she can't see me right now because she would probably take offense to the huge smile that I now have on my face. She's just too fucking cute for her own damn good. I swear it was her unwavering goodness and sweetness that was my total downfall. This may sound shitty but women come and go, but a sweet woman who just reeks of light and goodness is extremely rare in today's world.

Plus, I might have a thing for the whole kindergarten teacher thing. My mom was a teacher and my dad a cop. I wouldn't mind following in their footsteps. It's seemed to have worked out for them for close to forty years now.

Two of my sisters married fire fighters, I think just to annoy our dad. Okay they might not have married them to annoy him but they definitely agreed to the first date for that reason, I would bet a year's salary on it. At least two of them found quality guys, now if our baby sister Kellie could stop dating douchebags and ending up with deadbeat dads, that would be awesome.

I push the phone even closer to my ear like it could somehow place me right next to her. "I'm doing good honey. I was just wondering what you were up to right now?"

I learned that it's somewhat best to catch her off guard at times. Sage even told me it's best not to give her too much time to over think things.

"What!? Why!?" She screeches into the phone. I even have to pull it away a bit due to the volume that she just reached. I'm pretty sure the dogs down the street are now howling. "Ahem, I mean why would you like to know what I'm doing right now?"

She answers the second time more calmly but her voice is almost robotic. I can't understand why me asking her what she's doing would throw her into such a tizzy as my mother would say. Damn, she's even more skittish than I realized.

"I just wanted to see if you were busy right now. I've been craving a big greasy burger all day. Especially since I had to skip lunch because of a call. The diner in town has some of the best ones. I was just wondering if you wanted to have dinner with me there...tonight?"

I cringe at my words. Even I would turn me down after that long ass rant. Jesus man, what happened to keeping it quick and simple?

"Oh." She says in her low, angelic voice. "Umm," I can imagine her worrying her bottom lip with her teeth as she normally does as she speaks. "I suppose so."

Jumping up I pump my fist in the air. "But..." Dammit...so close. "I will need to be home early. I have school tomorrow and I like to get an adequate amount of sleep. It helps being aware and alert when dealing with small children." She states primly.

I smile the biggest smile that I think has ever come across my face. "I wouldn't dream of keeping you out late on a school night sweetheart. Don't worry, I'll make sure that you're in bed at an early hour."

I hear her making a choking/coughing sound on the other end of the line. I know that I should probably tread lightly but I just really couldn't help myself. My mouth started speaking before my brain was able to tell it to shut the fuck up. Please do not let me have screwed it up before it even began.

She's talking again "Ah, umm, yes, I would appreciate, ahem, being home at a decent hour. Thank you. I could even just meet you there so that I can leave if you feel like staying out later!" She practically shouts that last part out a little too excitedly.

I snigger to myself and sit up, yeah that shit ain't happening. I'm getting as much time with her as I possibly can. Even if it just means me picking her up and dropping her off at home. Grabbing the *Sports Illustrated* magazine from the table I stare into Peyton Manning's smiling face as I answer. "No, I like going to bed early myself on work nights." This is a lie, I'm a night owl, but she doesn't need to know that just yet.

"It will work out just fine if I pick you up. Plus, there have been a few muggings in town – okay one – and I would just feel better knowing that you were safe at all times." Yeah, yeah, yeah, I know that I'm going to hell for preying on her fear like this, but it's been fucking months! Desperate times call for desperate measures.

"Oh my gosh!" She gasps. I just smile, she doesn't even curse fully. "I hadn't heard about that." She pauses again and I just know that she's chewing on the damn bottom lip that is quickly becoming somewhat of an obsession of mine. "Well, if you think that it would be best for you to pick me up then I guess you should. You're the police officer after all, you would know best when it comes to safety issues."

"I really do think that it would be best." Straight to hell, my ass isn't even going to pass go, just straight down.

"Well, okay then. Do you think that you could give me an hour or so? I need to run to the store to pick something up." She says.

Tossing the magazine down I lean back.

"Why don't we just stop while we're in town. It doesn't make sense to have you drive into town to go to the store when we'll be there soon anyway." I plan to get as much time in with her as possible.

"Ahhhh, it's kind of a personal matter type of thing that I need to pick up." I just smile and shake my head.

"Sweetheart, I have three sisters. I have no problem with spending a few minutes in the tampon aisle. Hell, I've even had to go in by myself and pick some up for them."

I can hear her blow out a big breath. Crap, maybe she's not comfortable with that? "Or, I could just wait in the car while you go inside. Whatever makes you more comfortable."

"Yes, that would probably be for the best." I shrug to myself at her words.

"Alright, so how about I pick you up in like twenty minutes? Is that okay?" I ask hopefully. Like Sage said, the less time she has to think, the better.

"Yes, that's fine. Do you need my address?" She asks sweetly.

"Nope, it's a small town and Declan pointed it out one day when we were on patrol together." Not a total lie. I did get her address from him. It doesn't count as stalking if I'm on patrol and making my rounds around town. If I happen to pass the school and her house a few times, it just means that I'm thorough. Call it doing my job!

"Oh, okay. That makes sense. He's driven me home from Sage's house a few times." Lucky bastard.

"Okay sweetheart, I'll see you in a few then."

"Okay, bye Rocco."

I miss her voice immediately when the call is ended. But I'm happy with the arrangements. Scrolling through my phone I click the connect button to one of my favorite people in the world. The fact that she happens to know Lavender is just a bonus.

"Hello big brother. What do I owe the pleasure of this phone call to?" Amy asks on the third ring. The pecking order in our family goes Rachel, me, Amy and then Kellie. Even though I'm only two and half years older than her, she never lets me forget it.

"Well hello to you too. Can't a guy just call his sister to check in?" I pretend to be offended.

She snickers loudly. "You already did your check in text earlier, so I know that you either want or need something. So, fess up big brother because I have three trouble making children and I need to find a way to legally sell their misbehaving butts!"

I smirk and shake my head. She is the epitome of a great mom. But damn is she strict. Knowing her, they probably just forgot to put away a few toys and now she's annoyed. I love her but her need for complete order is insane. I feel bad for her husband Zach. Poor guy just randomly starts cleaning shit nowadays after being married to her OCD ass for so many years now.

"What did they do? Leave a cap off a marker?" I fake a gasp. "Did they not brush their teeth for a full two minutes? Oh wait, did they forget to put their dishes in the sink properly?" I chuckle. I can just picture her scowling at me through the phone.

"No, you jerk, the girls went through all of my makeup and put it all over Nicholas!" She screeches.

"Did they do a good job and make him look pretty?" I just know that I'm going to *"accidentally"* get hit in the nuts the next time that I see her but it's worth it to get on her nerves.

"That's not the point Rocco Anthony!" I squeeze my eyes shut at the sound of my middle name. "Do you have any idea how expensive all of that makeup is?" At my silence she just sighs. "Plus, Nicholas is only two. He keeps running away from me every time I get near him with a makeup remover wipe."

I smile, making sure to hold in the laugh that is dying to come out. I can just picture Nick looking like a damn clown and running all over the house to get away from Amy. Damn, I wish the girls were old enough to video stuff like this for the rest of the family to enjoy.

"So, what do you want butthead, I'm busy?!" She says in her best sassy attitude. Which really isn't that much. The other two are the brats in the family. Amy is just neurotic...in a nice way.

"Ouch. No need for name calling. Aren't you supposed to set a good example for your kids?"

"They're in the other room because I've given up and am either going to sell them or wait for Zach to take care of it. Now, why did you call?" She asks again

I decide to show her some mercy. She sounds seconds away from downing a bottle of wine. "So, I've convinced Lavender to come and have dinner with me tonight." There's a loud screech on the other end.

"Really?! Wow! I can't believe it! Seriously."

I frown into the phone. "Why do you say it like that? I'm not that bad."

"No, no dummy, that's not what I meant. Even when we were in school together, she was always really quiet. It didn't help that some of the idiots would make fun of her for having a teenage mother as a sister. I swear, kids are just so damn dumb at times."

I file that away for later. I know with Amy and I only being a little over two years apart, you would think that I would remember Lavender, but I just don't. Though if it wasn't football, my family or joining the Navy, I didn't really give anything else too much attention. I'm kicking myself for that now though.

"Okay, so then why are you so surprised that she said yes to me now?" I intentionally leave out the Vegas part

"Well, because after her bad breakup with Derek, she really hasn't dated all that much." Amy's talking again "Not that I can blame her. That guy is such an asshole and was always so mean to her any time I saw them together. I just figured that she would be cautious. But I'm so happy that she's giving you a chance."

I have to bite my fist to keep from growling at the news. "I didn't know that she just got out of a relationship?" I try for casual but fail miserably.

"Hmm, it was a few years ago actually. I think it was right around the time that you had just gotten back from the Navy and started working at the Police Department. So, what, that's about four years now...right?"

I grunt. "Yeah, about that. So, she seriously hasn't dated anyone since this *Derek* guy?" I spit his name out like a curse.

"I think she's gone on a few dates but nothing has ever come from them. Honestly, I think he did a number on her. Plus the jackass, literally got married to some chick like three months after they broke up and started popping out a bunch of kids. That can't be easy to see, especially since even I've noticed that he always makes sure that she sees them. I kind of want to trip him when he's walking across the street and a car is coming."

I just smile into the phone. Amy may be the sweet one but she doesn't like when others are being treated badly. And as I've recently found out, her and Lavender have always been friendly. "He sounds like a real winner." I drawl.

"Yeah, not so much. I guess they met in college. Sage didn't even meet him for like the first two years. And then afterwards it was obvious that she hated him with a damn passion. Derek was never anywhere that Sage and/or Danny were." She snickers loudly. "Especially Danny." She chuckles.

I smirk because yeah, I wouldn't really want to be on his bad side either. I also need to make a note of asking Sage a little more about this guy. Like his last name and license plate number. It's not my fault if Declan and Marc have been itching for some new fun.

I glance at my watch and notice it's almost time. "I just called to see if you had any advice for me. I need to leave in like two minutes to go get her." The conversation lasted longer than I anticipated but at least I found out a few more details about Lavender than originally.

"Just be gentle and go slowly with her." Too late I think to myself but don't voice for obvious reasons. "Also, just be really nice. I swear the guy treated her like absolute crap and I don't think any of her other dates were much better. She is way too nice to be treated badly." I whole heartedly agree with that statement.

"Got it. Just be my awesomely charming and handsome self."

"Why don't you take it down a few notches Casanova? You don't need to scare her away."

"Fine, point taken. I'll try to conceal some of my sexiness." The gag that I hear on the other end of the phone is extremely satisfying.

"Ah, do not make me sick. We had spaghetti for dinner and I do not need that coming back up."

"Thanks for the visual." I drawl.

"You're so very welcome." She chirps like a brat. "Like I said, be sweet and don't be bossy like you always are."

I snort. "I'm only bossy with you three."

"Right." She chuckles. "Good luck big brother. Text me and let me know how it goes!" She squeals. I have a feeling that within two minutes every member of my family is going to know that I'm taking Lavender out tonight. Like she reads my mind she responds "Hey and don't worry about Rach and Kel mentioning anything to Ma."

Relieved I sigh.

"You're my favorite." It's not exactly a lie.

"Duh, I'm the most awesome one. Of course, I'm your favorite." She laughs.

"Night brat, thanks for the advice."

"Just try not to screw it up and get her to agree to a second date...will ya?"

"That's the plan sis."

Oh no, what in the world did I just agree to? I can't go out to dinner with him! Firstly, because I can't form coherent thoughts or words when I'm in his presence. And there won't even be anyone else that I can use as a buffer so that I don't have to interact with him.

Secondly, the last thing I need is for him to go to the store with me and see me picking up a pregnancy test. I mean he did say he would stay in the car. But what if I drop the bag and the test falls out? What if he thinks I'm some kind of easy girl who just sleeps with anyone? Or worse, that I'm pregnant with his kid!

Third...well. I just can't do this. What if he turns out to be a total jerk just like every other man that I have ever met? Sure, all the guys that JJ works with are nothing but big old softies. Well, maybe not Damon, except for whenever I see him with Michelle and Jax, he's really sweet to them.

But what if Rocco is the only jerk out of the group? That will just kill all my fantasies and dreams! And honestly, that's really all I have going for me in the love life department right now. The thought of him is probably much better than reality. I should definitely call him back and cancel. A stomach bug is totally reasonable since I work with little germ factories. It's sounds completely plausible.

I swear it's almost as if she has some weird radar for when I'm having a freak out. I look down at my ringing phone and see that it's Sage. I answer immediately and regret every ounce of word vomit that spews from me the second it comes out.

"I slept with Rocco in Vegas because of your stupid wedding and those stupid tequila shots. I've been avoiding him ever since. I took a pregnancy test, I'm pregnant, or so it lies, it's one hundred percent his, if the stupid test isn't lying. He called, I answered and agreed to have dinner with him. I told him that I needed to stop at the store before we go to dinner and he said that he would take me." When she doesn't say anything I continue.

"He even said that he would stay in the car when he thought that I needed to go get tampons. But I'm going in to get like four other brands of tests because this has to be a lie because I'm not able to get pregnant."

My eyes dart to the pregnancy test on the sink. "Now I'm scared that the test will fall out of the bag and he'll either think that I'm a whore – which I kind of am for having sex with him in the first place – or that it's his which is even worse. I'm also scared that I'll tell him that I'm pregnant and he'll freak out and yell at me." At the end I suck in a huge gulp of air.

"Umm, hi." Sage says uncertainly.

"That's all you have to say? Hi?!" I screech. "After everything I just said!"

"It's a lot of information to process in a few seconds. Do you think that you could give me a minute?" She asks reasonably and any other time I would be more than happy to oblige.

"No! Didn't you hear me, he's on his way over to pick me up now! I need advice and fast!"

"What are you wearing?" She asks like a crazy person.

"Why does it matter what I'm wearing?"

"Well, because if I know you as well as I think I do, you came home from work and put on pajamas. I don't think flannel pajamas with hearts all over them are going to be appropriate to wear to dinner." She drawls.

I gasp when I look down and realize that she's right. She even got the design correct, not that I'll be admitting that to her smug butt. "Crud!" I shout before getting off the bathroom floor and running into my bedroom. Everything happens in slow motion one minute I'm up, the next my feet are slipping from under me sending me crashing to the floor.

"Oww." I say and rub my forehead.

"What happened?" I can hear the laughter in her voice, the evil witch.

"I ran into the door frame face first because I slipped on the floor." I wonder if that would be good enough reason to cancel the date?

"Don't even think about it!" She literally growls at me. "You're going out with him and that's it. He's a great guy who really likes you. He also might be your baby daddy, so you should probably give him a shot...just saying."

"Have you heard nothing that I've said?"

"I've heard every wonderful word my tequila slutty sister. And in all honesty, I thought you would be really happy to be pregnant since you were told that you might not be able to have children at all."

I sigh and realize that she's right. I have PCOS or Polycystic Ovarian Syndrome and Endometriosis. My body is just a ball of womanly hatred for me. My doctor said that I had a slim to none chance of ever becoming pregnant. I found out that wonderful gem while I was dating Derek who promptly broke up with me for being *"a defective woman"* as he so eloquently put it. I know that I should be ecstatic and worried, but a doctors visit will help with the worry.

"I am...sort of. You've seen me around him." I ignore her rude snort and continue. "How am I supposed to raise a child with a man that I'm not in a relationship with and one that I can barely talk to?"

"Well, it seems to me like he's trying to fix that relationship issue by asking you out. You're going to have to find your lady balls and learn how to talk to the man that you like and dream about getting sweaty between the sheets with." She laughs. "Opps, too late." She starts cackling again sounding more like an evil witch.

"You're supposed to be helping me." I whine like the little sister that I am. It's her job to solve all my boy problems, regardless of our age.

"Wear tight jeans that show off your curves and butt. A cute top but not overly sexy and some booties. That way you look casual but still hot....just not like you're trying too hard."

"That's really not what I was hoping for." But useful as I rummage through my closet. Still won't be admitting that to her either.

"Sorry Lav, you got yourself into this mess. Now you need to be a big girl and go on a date with your baby daddy." She starts laughing like a hyena again. "But hey, if it's any consolation, I'm preggers too, so we can at least be fat and miserable together."

I frown at my phone. "I thought JJ got a vasectomy?"

"He didn't before our wedding." She says in a droll voice making me snort.

"I guess I'm not the only tequila slutty one." I chirp.

"Yeah but I'm married to mine. You're trying to figure out how to even talk to yours."

"You can't say anything!" I shout out randomly.

"Umm, Lav, sweetie, I hate to break it to you, but people are going to notice a huge basketball shape in front of you. Even men aren't that oblivious."

"I get that Sage, I'm not dumb. But I need to at least visit the doctor to make sure everything is fine first. Why would I tell him when it probably won't work out anyway." I say quietly.

"Lav, don't think like that honey. You don't know that anything will be wrong. Maybe this was just meant to be and that's why you were able to get all knocked up. Vegas can be magical when it comes to sperm."

"This conversation is taking a very odd turn." I tell her.

"Yeah, I took the tests a few days ago and told JJ. Ever since then my mind has been on his overachieving swimmers and Vegas. But I promise not to say anything to anyone until you get everything checked out."

I let out a sigh. "Thank you."

"You're welcome. Now get dressed, look cute and go have a fun dinner with your baby daddy." She laughs before hanging up.

I just shake my head at the phone. Out of the two of us, she definitely inherited more traits from our parents than I did. I chuckle to myself. They would probably be happy to know that I had a one-night stand and ended up pregnant. They are wonderful parents but so very strange.

Also, does it count as a one-night stand if you go out on a date with them afterwards? Ah, I don't even know the rules of the whole dating and sleeping with someone thing. The only person that I've ever been with was Derek and we dated for months before we had sex. I wish that I had never met him. If only I could go back in time and run in the opposite direction when I first saw him.

Forcing thoughts of him to the back of my mind I try to focus on more positive things like what I'm going to wear.

I pull out a cute outfit from my closet. Tight skinny dark blue jeans, a somewhat lowcut black top and my black booties. I throw it all on in record time. I'm just adding some bracelets and earrings when, at the sound of the doorbell I jump, slightly stabbing myself with my earring.

I slow run to the door and come to a complete halt before placing my hand on the doorknob. Taking a deep breath I tell myself that once I open this door, everything changes. Okay, yeah, I know, I'm pregnant – maybe not – with the man's baby. But until I open this door, I can totally stay in my perfect little bubble of denial. My mind wrestles with the decision. Is it so wrong for me to want to keep my life the way it was before I peed on that stupid stick?

Okay, okay, I can do this. I just have to do as Sage said and find my lady balls. I think that they're probably shriveled up in utter fear right now but whatever. I am a grown woman and I can most certainly handle going on a date with a man that I may or may not have seen naked.

I jump again when he rings the doorbell for a second time. Shoot! Right I need to be an adult and open the door. No more hiding in my little bubble. I take a deep breath and open the door. The air immediately leaves my lungs when I see him.

Good Lord, one man should not be able to make a light green T-shirt and light blue jeans look so darn tempting. Even his face is perfect! Sparkling hazel eyes, dirty blonde hair that looks like he just ran his hand through it, a day's worth of yummy scruff and a huge smile directed right at me.

If I died right now with him smiling at me like this, I would die a very happy woman. I'd die happier if I could remember what he looked like naked, but I'll take what I can get.

"Hi gorgeous, you ready to go?" He says in his deep, yet gentle voice.

I nod dumbly at him as I try to force my brain to regain function. You can think thoughts....please put them to use!

His smile gets even wider. "Do you have everything or do you need to get your purse?"

Blinking a few times I shake my head. "Right! Yes, I mean, yes, I need to get my purse. I'll just be one moment," I stammer

I turn swiftly and power walk to the kitchen counter where I left my purse when I got home from work. I take out my keys so that I can lock my door and turn on my heel. I stop dead in my tracks when I see Rocco just standing there staring at me. "What?" I ask nervously while biting my bottom lip. It's a nervous habit that I really need to break.

He gives me a smirk that goes straight from my belly down to my core. Oh boy, I am in so much trouble around him. "Nothing at all sweetheart. I was just admiring the view."

I can feel my face flame at his words. Yup, so much trouble. "Umm, okay." Please, brain, for me, please come back online for just a little bit tonight. I really don't want this man thinking that I'm a complete and utter moron.

He nods towards my purse and keys, that I have luckily not dropped upon his unashamed perusal of my body. "You have everything that you need now?"

"Yes, I'm ready to go now." I whisper. Well, at least I'm speaking. That's a start. I'll deal with my volume later.

He gives me another bright smile and holds the door open for me. "After you."

I look up – way up – as I pass him and smile shyly. "Thank you."

We walk down the walkway towards his truck and he keeps his hand at the small of my back the entire time. I can feel the heat of his hand searing into me, almost like he's branding me with just a simple touch. He clicks the lock and opens the door for me and holds out his hand. I tilt my head and raise an eyebrow in question.

He gives me a small smile. "Anytime I drive my mom or my sisters anywhere, they always need help getting in." He shrugs like one of my students right before they do something naughty. "I figured that you might not appreciate me picking you up and placing you inside."

I swallow all the saliva pooling in my mouth. He has no idea how much I really wouldn't mind that at all. His touch is potent and bad for us right now. "Do you pick up your mom and sisters and place them inside your truck usually?"

"My momma, no I just give her my arms to hold onto." He shrugs like a little boy again and gets a wicked smirk. "My sisters might get a little helping *push* inside. I'm a good brother like that."

I can't even help the embarrassing snort that comes out of me. "Yes, I'm sure that you're so very helpful to them."

The goofball grabs his chest and gives me a look of mock shock. "I can't believe that you don't believe that I am the world's best brother. Those three brats absolutely worship the ground that I walk on."

"You do realize that I know two of your sisters...right?" I sass, surprised that I'm no longer tongue tied.

"Whatever they've said is a complete lie. The two youngest are always the worst in the family. You wouldn't believe how awful those two are." He says with a very somber face making me laugh.

"How about I just use your arm to hoist myself up like your momma does?"

"Anything that you want sweetheart." His words come out breezily, but I feel like there is a double meaning hidden in there somewhere.

I ignore that and grab onto his muscular arm. I can feel his veins protruding through his shirt. Eventually I lift myself up into the passenger seat of his truck.

"Don't forget to buckle up." He says with a wink before shutting the door and sauntering over to the driver's side. And that's the only way to describe his walk.

I knew that he was making sure that I got a good view of him. Not that I was complaining about it. Staring at his glorious muscly body is one of my favorite pastimes. I should probably start looking into new hobbies that don't involve him in any sort of way.

Once inside Rocco fastens his seatbelt and starts the truck up. He looks over at me with those mesmerizing hazel eyes, eyes that I wouldn't mind staring into forever. "You ready?" He asks with an almost secretive smirk. Like he knows something that I don't.

Again I get the feeling that he's asking more than just a simple question. I want to chuckle with the thought that he thinks he's the one with a secret. Oh, boy – or girl - if he only knew, he probably wouldn't be smirking so much. I just smile in return and nod my head. "Yup, I'm all ready to go now."

S o that's how to get her talking to me with ease. She relaxes every time I'm even the least bit silly. All throughout dinner anytime she would start chewing on that gloriously full bottom lip, I would realize that she was starting to get nervous again. But anytime I said or did anything funny or silly, she would automatically relax.

But I hopefully have time to figure all of that out. We're back in my truck driving to the store. A weird tenseness has come over her. She's sitting ram rod straight and gnawing on her lip like it will help find the cure for cancer. It's weird that she's so freaked out that I know that she needs tampons. I mean it's a normal part of life.

Once I put the truck in park, I notice that she makes absolutely no move to get out. She actually appears to be shaking. When she turns her head and looks at me there are tears in her eyes. What the fuck is going on?

"I'm pregnant!" She half shouts and half blurts out. I don't even have time to respond before she continues, though that's probably a good thing because right now I've got nothing.

"Stupid Vegas and tequila. I'm not normally like that...you know?" She looks over at me, those chocolate eyes swimming in tears and all I can do is nod my head yes, because I do know that. I'm also getting a funny feeling about where this is going.

I'm trying hard to wrap my mind around what she is saying but she just keeps going.

"And okay so it looked kind of bad when I woke up naked and in bed with you. And okay, sure I was sore in areas that hadn't been sore in years. But I figured maybe I rode one of those mechanical bulls that they have in like every bar in the universe."

Finally I'm able to get a word in. "You haven't been to a lot of bars, have you?"

She looks taken aback for a moment before recovering and shaking her head. "No, I barely drink wine and that's only when I'm with Sage and Kay...oh and Dee. She really can be such a horrible influence." I just smirk because there is no disagreeing with that.

"Anyway," she continues "I figured that it was just some weird dream thing and decided to forget about it." Well if that isn't a major hit to my ego. Damn, handing her a knife would've been less painful.

"And lets just be real here. I can barely talk to you normally without embarrassing myself. And I look nothing like the women who are constantly throwing themselves at you. So, I figured that whatever happened that night in Vegas would just stay there like the saying. Only, I took a test right before you called me and it came back positive. But I think it's one of those false positive things because I was told that my chances of having children are very slim to like none."

I listen to her explain how she took a test and it came back positive. Even as she talks about it, I can hear the uncertainty in her voice. I on the other hand am still reeling from the announcement. I try to focus on her words, but the only thing I can hear is pregnant.

"When you called, I was trying to convince myself to get off my bathroom floor and go and get more tests so that I could prove that the other one was a big fat liar. Then you called and my brain stopped working and I stupidly said yes to dinner and letting you take me to the store. And I figured that I might as well tell you about this now because I'm pretty sure that with my luck I would trip and all of the boxes of pregnancy tests that I plan on buying would go sailing into the air and probably land in your lap. And the last thing that I want is for you to think that I'm some floozy who needs to buy so many tests because she's out tramping it up."

I rub a hand down my face. Holy shit that was a lot of information in a short amount of time. If I'm understanding her correctly, she's pregnant with my child.

"You okay over there?" I ask gently since she's still breathing heavily.

She's looking down at her intertwined fingers. "If I asked you to just kill me now, is there any chance that you would do it?" She asks in an embarrassed and pleading voice.

I smirk at her even though she isn't looking at me. "It would probably look pretty bad to kill the mother of my child, don't you think?"

Her head whips up and her eyes are wide. And if I'm not mistaken a little frightened too. "You caught that part, huh?"

I nod my head seriously. "Yeah, that part stuck out a bit."

"Darn." I hear her whisper to herself. She looks at me with those chocolate orbs filled with tears. "I'm so sorry. I don't even know how this happened. I swear I didn't plan for any of this. I really didn't even think that I would ever be able to get pregnant. This was the last thing that I ever expected." She finished up her mini rant sobbing.

Unable to take it, I unbuckle both of our seatbelts and pull her into my lap. I wrap my arms around her and place her head in the crook of my neck while she just sobs and says how sorry she is.

"Shh, sweetheart, it will be okay. And I'm pretty sure that I played a decent role in that night myself. We'll figure this out honey, it's not the end of the world. If anything, the world will be gaining a great looking kid." I joke hoping to make her laugh.

She looks up at me with those eyes so wide. "You're not mad at me?"

I blink a few times surprised. "Sweetheart, why would I be mad at you? We both drank our weight in tequila and most likely didn't use protection. It's no one's fault but the tequilas and possibly Declan."

She sits back with a shocked look on her face. "You remember him pushing us into the elevator too right? I didn't just imagine that right?"

"No, my memory is fuzzy at best, but I do remember him and a big ass grin on his face. It's safe to say that if we really wanted to, we could place all the blame on him and everyone would go along with it."

"I'm going to wring his neck." She says in the most adorable growl that I've ever heard. I just raise an eyebrow at her and she gives me a sheepish look. "Okay, fine, I'll get Sage and Kayla to do my dirty work for me. It's not my fault that they're really good at it."

She's not wrong. "So, how about it sweetheart? You ready to go in there, buy a bunch of tests and find out if were about to have the world's most genetically gifted child?"

She blinks at me a few times. "You do realize that since we don't have any similar traits like eyes or hair color, that our child could come out looking like *Mister Ed* or that *Chucky Doll*...right?"

I shake my head. "I refuse to believe that. We're both ridiculously good looking. There's no way our child could be anything less than extraordinary."

She snorts like a little mini pig, not that I'll be telling her that, I like my nuts right where they are. "You're ridiculously good looking. I'm average at best."

I narrow my eyes at the crazy woman most likely carrying my child. "Yeah, we'll be having a nice long conversation about certain things later. Like how you don't realize how perfect you are. But right now we have more important things to do. Like buy sticks for you to pee on."

She gives me an odd look. "You're even weirder than Amy has said." There goes her favorite status...damn traitor.

"I've already told you not to believe anything my bratty sisters say." I open my door and drag us both out. "Now quit stalling and let's go. We have eighty million pregnancy test brands to look at."

I grab her hand in mine and start walking her towards the entrance. "There aren't that many."

I look down at her briefly. "How can you say that? They have an entire aisle full of them."

She shakes her head as we make our way through the store. "No, they share the aisle with condoms. You know the things that our drunk butts should've remembered to use?"

"Do you ever curse?" She stumbles a bit. I smile inwardly liking that I can catch her off guard.

She glares up at me. "No, I work with small children. The last thing I need is to say a bad word and have one of them repeat it at home. They're like sponges. And they're listening even when you think that they aren't."

I smirk at her once more. "Did you even curse before becoming a teacher?"

"No, because I've always known what I wanted to do with my life, even when I was a little girl." She sniffs and keeps walking.

I am so damn screwed. She is literal perfection and she's probably carrying my baby right now. I should probably be freaking out about this, but instead I'm oddly happy. First, I love kids. I love being an uncle, so I can only imagine how much I'm going to love being a father.

Second, it's almost like fate has literally fucking threw her into my arms and said *"Here you go. She's all yours."* It's not the best way to start a relationship, but if she is pregnant, it means that she can't pull that annoying ass disappearing act on me.

She'll have to see and talk to me. And if she happens to fall madly in love with me and decides to have all of my babies, well who am I to stop her?

"Which ones should we get?" She asks me like I would know.

I look down and shrug. "One of each, I guess." They can't all be wrong.

She blows out a breath. "Okay, one of each it is."

I can't believe they all came back positive. I really never thought that I would be able to get pregnant but according to a few dozen tests, I most definitely am pregnant.

It was absolutely in no way awkward taking all of those tests while Rocco was in the next room. I suppose that it was better than what he originally proposed, him being inside the bathroom with me. I decided to just pee in a plastic cup and dunk all of the tests in. But still, there was no way that I was going to let him see a cup filled with my pee.

Besides my word vomit – for the second time that evening – I was still not really able to speak to him. Well, I was but not in totally coherent ways all of the time. So, yes, I made him stay in the living room until I had everything finished and cleaned up, much to his chagrin.

Once I walked back out into the living room we sat in extremely awkward silence until the timer that I set, started beeping. He got up first and held his hand out to me. I took it and he pulled me up off the couch and we walked hand in hand into the bathroom. There we saw that every stick was positive. We figured that they all couldn't be wrong.

I couldn't really tell what Rocco was thinking. He didn't seem upset but he didn't exactly seem excited either. He had more of a contemplative look on his face. I on the other hand was absolutely terrified. I never imagined this happening, especially with the one man who makes me too nervous to function.

We sat on my couch talking the entire night. I found that I eventually could use full sentences around him – yay me – when we were discussing important issues. I thought that it was odd that he didn't immediately ask me if I wanted to keep the baby and told him so.

He started laughing so hard that he had tears streaming down his face. I didn't really understand what was so funny until he finally calmed down. I also didn't really care all that much because he has a great laugh and my traitorous hormones were enjoying watching his muscles moving.

He explained to me that he comes from an Irish and Italian family – it explains why he's blonde with hazel eyes and his sisters all have dark hair and brown eyes- and that not keeping the baby isn't even a thought that he would entertain. He even said that if I truly didn't want the baby that he would just raise the baby all on his own. I might have swooned a tiny bit hearing that, not that I'll admit that to anyone, including myself.

So, then we had to have the just wonderful conversation about how I never thought that I would be able to have children. I explained that I was told that due to certain factors – that he annoyingly made me explain in detail – that it might not be possible for me to conceive. I unfortunately even had to go into my relationship and subsequent end of my relationship with Derek.

I swear I have never wanted to hide under a rock more than I did when I had to explain to the absolutely gorgeous Adonis sitting next to me that he was my second sexual partner. I couldn't even look at him during that conversation, I literally had a pillow close to my face. I did catch a weird grin at one point, but I wasn't really sure what it meant, so I just ignored it.

He told me that he's only dated two women within the last four years and that those were both short relationships. He also told me that it's been close to a year since he's been with anyone – I definitely gave him a skeptical look – and said that he's been tested since. He even said that he would give me a copy of his health records if I wanted them. I figured that was probably overkill, but a sweet offer.

So, here we sit a few weeks later at my OB-GYN's office, waiting on my first appointment. Apparently, you have to be a certain number of weeks along before you can be seen. That seems like a bad idea to someone who was told that they could never have children and has been freaking out since taking the test, but what do I know. I'm just the one having a small mental breakdown...no biggie.

One thing that has been a weird new thing in my life, besides the whole pregnant thing, is that Rocco has seemed to make himself a permanent fixture in my life. My sister being the good sister that she is, hasn't told anyone that I'm pregnant and Rocco promised me the same.

Though, now everyone thinks that Rocco and I are dating. Something that I've tried to explain otherwise, but got roadblocked by my apparent *"boyfriend"* or *"my man"* - his words – telling everyone that we know, that we are indeed a couple.

After that, everyone ignored my protests, even my own traitor family members. I even tried to complain to Rocco's sister Amy and just became even more frustrated with that conversation when she welcomed me to her family. It's like every single person around me has lost their ever-loving minds!

I guess I understand why he told them that we're a couple, since he's been spending so much time with me. But he could've just said that we're friends. It's almost like he's enjoying the fact that no one will listen to my protests. I swear every time I look at him, he has a weird, contemplative look on his face.

I am not even going to get into how he has inserted himself into every facet of my life. He has even started bringing me lunch and sitting with me, even if he's on duty. I feel like that is probably a terrible misuse of tax payer money.

He comes over every night...I repeat every night. Do you have any idea what it's like to have your hormones going all crazy and having your fantasy with you constantly. It's torture, plain and simple.

I can't even explain how close to a total breakdown I came when he came back from the gym all sweaty and showered at my house. I'm not even going to lie about standing near the door and trying to hear every second of the time he spent naked in the same shower that I use.

I've come so close to mauling the poor man a few times that I've had to physically move myself away from him. It's almost like he knows that he's my darn catnip and is trying his hardest to make me a kitty junkie.

Of course, Sage is absolutely no help with her telling me to jump him every time that I talk to her. I figure that at this point, it's best to not talk to her about him at all.

So, here we sit waiting to be seen. The longer we sit here the more annoyed I become as well. I no longer seem to be emotionally stable because I'm ready to gouge someone's eyes out. Every woman in this place, has been staring at Rocco like he's a juicy piece of steak. Even the hugely pregnant women, who are sitting next to their significant others, are drooling.

I mean, sure, we're in a sort of – fakeish – relationship, so that would totally give me the right to give these women a nasty look right? They don't know that we aren't madly in love and getting married. Awful heifers. And Rocco is just sitting here on his phone oblivious to the fact that he might be arresting the mother of his child for murder soon.

Geez, I need to calm myself down. He's not really yours Lav, I say to myself no matter how many people think otherwise. Just take a nice deep breath in and let it all out, along with the urge to maim every other woman in this place.

"Are you meditating?" I jump at the sound of Rocco's question against my right ear.

I look up at him and give him a smile that I'm pretty sure that serials killers wear. "Yeah, I thought that I might start to do that." I need to not to kill someone.

He nods his head with a smile. "Great idea. I was reading up on pregnancy the other night and read that mediating is great for you and the baby. Keeping your stress levels down will do a lot of good for the two of you."

And there goes another tiny piece of my heart that this man shouldn't have. At some point he's going to realize that average me isn't good enough. And if things keep going the way they're going, I'm going to be completely in love with him and end up totally devastated. I have a feeling it will be a thousand times worse than my break up with Derek ever was.

"You've been reading up about pregnancy?" I blink a few times.

He gives me a look that I can't one hundred percent decipher, but if I had to take a guess he's mentally calling me an idiot, but he's too sweet to say it out loud. "Yes, why wouldn't I? I want to make sure that I can be as helpful as possible to you throughout this whole pregnancy. We're in this together...remember?" He nudges me with his shoulder.

Chip, chip, chip, there goes even more pieces. I don't think that I'll ever be completely whole again. I give him a smile that I know looks strained because it is. "Right, definitely in this together."

He gives me a dubious look but goes back to looking at his phone.

"Lavender?" Is called from a side door, by a very blonde woman wearing tight pink scrubs. I hear a few snickers in regards to my name, but that's nothing new. Thanks Mom and Dad.

Rocco and I both stand and walk towards the woman who called my named. When she gets a look at Rocco, she literally licks her lips. Deep breaths in and out Lav, I remind myself it wouldn't be good to have a baby in prison.

"Right this way." She purrs looking at Rocco and completely ignoring me, you know, the pregnant one. When she does look at me, she gives me a grimace like she can't believe that a guy who looks like Rocco is with someone who looks like me. You and me both girl.

"We need to get your height and weight. If you could just step up here please." She says in a nasty voice. Too bad for her that I may have curves but I'm five feet, seven inches tall. I don't weight all that much.

You can tell that she's disappointed too when she sees the number on the scale. I snigger quietly to myself. I really do have a decent body type and have never had any issues with my weight. Which is pretty incredible, since uncontrollable weight gain is one of the symptoms of PCOS. I actually wonder sometimes if I would be severely underweight if I didn't have the condition.

Barbie, as I'll call her, since her rude butt didn't introduce herself, looks me over again. "If *you*" – she somewhat hisses out – "and your....." She's now looking up at Rocco batting her eyelashes. Good grief, have some self-respect, he's good looking, not Tom Hardy.

"Her man." Rocco answers in a weird sort of growl that I've never heard from him before.

Even Barbie seems to be taken off guard because she walks us straight to a room without another word. She tells me to undress and put on the weird paper gown and high tails it out as fast as she possibly can.

I look at Rocco and blink a few times before tilting my head in question. He shrugs unapologetically at me. "What? She was annoying and rude. We're here about a pregnancy and she's trying to flirt with me. I don't have patience for that shit."

"Crud." I automatically blurt out. Ignoring the way my heart is doing a little happy dance that he had absolutely no interest in her. I can be petty if I want. I'm pregnant and hormonal. I plan to ride this wave as long as I can, thank you very much.

He looks at me with a blank look. "What?"

"You need to start saying crud instead of the S word." I explain. "Actually, we probably need to start getting you to curb all of your bad language usage now, before the baby gets here."

He's looking at me like I'm insane. I snicker mentally, he's the one who wanted me to start talking to him more. You should always be careful what you wish for. With him spending so much time with me, I've been able to become somewhat accustomed to him.

I don't count when he's shirtless, any woman's eyes would get flustered around all of that muscly goodness. But in general, I've come a long way. I have a feeling that he might be regretting that now.

"We need to curb my bad language...now?" He says slowly with wide eyes like he's uncertain about how to proceed with this conversation.

He's even taken a step back from me and is leaning against the counter with his arms crossed. Kind of like he's actually trying to protect himself from this conversation. Good grief, it's not like I'm asking him to become a darn vegan or anything.

I nod slowly. "Yes, it would be best if you got into the habit of using good language now."

"But the baby isn't even close to being here yet. And even then, it's like two years before they start to understand what you're saying."

I roll my eyes. "Obviously, but even when the baby is in the womb, he or she can hear what we say. Wouldn't it be better to have our baby hearing good things instead of bad?"

"Are you fucking with me right now?"

I growl actually growl and take a few steps towards this infuriating man who refuses to leave my life. "It's not that difficult! All you have to do is change a few darn words." I really don't know what has come over me – we'll blame the awful hormones – but I actually poke him in the chest, his very firm chest. He looks down at my finger like I've grown a second head before giving me a wicked smirk. Uh-oh, I forgot that you're not supposed to poke bears.

"Did you just growl, yell and poke me sweetheart?" He still has that smirk in place and I'm suddenly getting a very bad feeling.

Not the 'I'm about to get mugged' feeling but the other one that says my heart and body are so screwed. Run, the logical part of my brain is yelling. Stay and let him do as he pleases, screams my hormones and other unmentionable areas.

"Ah, no." I try to lie. I try and take a step back but he grabs my arm that was still up poking him, and pulls me flush against his body.

"You know, it's not nice to lie." He whispers against my lips.

"It's not nice to be a butt head." I whisper back and immediately want to crawl under a rock and die.

He clucks his tongue at me. "Well that wasn't very nice. Maybe I should show your mouth how to be nice from now on." Is what he says before his lips come crashing down onto mine.

There is nothing soft or gentle about this kiss. He is owning me with just his lips and tongue and he's making sure that I know it too. With his lips branding my own and his tongue caressing mine, I feel as if he's trying to reach down into my very soul with this kiss. Like if he could, he would tattoo his name across my heart.

I don't even realize that I've grabbed onto the back of his head until he lifts me up and I tug hard to give more traction. Good grief, this man can kiss. With my legs wrapped around him, I can feel every inch of him through my yoga pants.

We're both so distracted by the kiss that we don't register the door opening, before it's too late. "Well, at least we know exactly how this miracle baby came to be." My sixty-something and very sweet male doctor, Doctor Piech chuckles.

Rocco and I pull apart instantly at the sound of his voice. It doesn't really help anything, since I'm still in his arms and his hands are on my butt. I guess it's better than still being lip locked.

Yeah, if I could just find a gigantic rock to crawl under that would be wonderful. I look into Rocco's eye's and see that they're swimming with mirth. "This isn't funny." I hiss at him. "I've known him since I was a little girl."

"Sweetheart," Rocco starts and chuckles a little, earning himself a glare from me. "you're in here today because you're pregnant. Did you think that he would believe that it was due to immaculate conception?"

"No." I growl for the second time in minutes. Geez, these hormones are no job. "But I didn't expect him to come in and see me mauling my..." I stop there at a loss for what to call him.

Rocco narrows his eyes at me. "Your man, we've established that I'm your man. Several times to be exact." He grunts.

I snicker out very loudly. "Says you, not me." I reply smugly.

Rocco narrows his eyes even more and growls at me. Opps, yeah, his is a lot better than mine.

I swear this is the most stubborn woman that I have ever met! Sweet, most definitely, but stubborn beyond belief. Her refusal to claim me as hers is starting to get on my nerves.

Okay granted, she was sort of forced into this corner, but damn, I didn't think that it would take her this long to come around.

And damned if I didn't notice her ass giving every woman who looked my way a dirty ass look. I pretended to be on my phone while studying her out of the corner of my eye.

She looked ready to slit that blonde chicks throat who was flirting with me when she brought us in. I would've let her keep at it a bit longer since I was enjoying Lavenders reaction, but for real, it was just too disrespectful to deal with. Seriously though, who hits on a pregnant woman's man right in front of her?

And now after spending every moment that I can with her, I finally have her right where she belongs and we get interrupted. Granted, I shouldn't be mouth fucking her in the doctor's office but damn, can't a guy catch a break?

Okay, fine, it's probably that the doctor, who looks like he might've been the one to deliver Lav, walked in. But I'm not too keen on setting her down right now. The poor old guy doesn't need any more of a show and unfortunately, I wore sweatpants today, instead of jeans. I don't want to scare the poor guy.

"Will you put me down already." She swats and hisses at me like a pissed off little kitten. Probably shouldn't tell her she looks more cute than scary.

"I will if you promise to stand directly in front of me." I murmur to her.

Her brows furrow. "Why would I need to stand in front of you?" She asks at a normal volume. I know that she isn't very experienced – I won't lie and say that I'm not fucking thrilled because I sure as hell am – but she cannot be this clueless.

The doctor chuckles again. "He wants you to stand in front of him so that I don't have to look at his boner while meeting him for the first time darling."

I would laugh at the shade of red that she's turning, if I wasn't sure that I'm probably close to turning the same exact shade. Damn this guy doesn't have a filter. This ought to be a fun couple of months.

"Oh." She says before looking down and then right back up. "Ah, so I just stand in front of you once you put me down?"

We hear a snort from the doorway. "How about this. Since you were too busy smooching to put your gown on, I leave and come back in a few minutes. That way my dear, you can get changed and your man, as he insists that he is, can get himself under control while having a seat in one of the chairs."

We both blink at the man and nod our heads in unison. He gives us a big smile. "Excellent, I'll be back in about five minutes. Does that work for the two of you?"

We both just nod again and he exits the room, closing the door behind him. I look at Lav and she looks back at me. I burst out laughing while she smacks her head into my chest.

"I cannot believe that just happened. I am so darn embarrassed." She mumbles into my shirt.

I chuckle. "It could've been worse."

She looks up at me skeptically. "How could that have been any worse?"

"You could've already been in the gown and have given him a show. Although, considering his line of work, I don't think that it would've shocked him too much."

"Will you just be quiet and put me down please?" Ah, here's Miss Prim and Proper again. Don't worry, I'll dirty you up again...very, very soon.

"If you say so." I pretend to pout but still gently lower her back to the ground. The minute she moves, my hands immediately miss holding onto that glorious ass.

Not too firm, but not too jiggly, just perfect. And all mine, despite what she says. I'll kill any motherfucker who comes near her. I swipe a hand down my face. Jesus, I'm starting to turn into Damon. That can't be good.

"Are you just going to stand there?" She asks me from across the room.

I blink a few times. "I plan on eventually sitting in the chair, why?"

She purses her lips like she's sucking on a lemon. "I meant, are you going to stand there while I'm getting changed?"

"I don't see why not. I've seen it all before, hence why we're here." She's too easy to bait.

"It doesn't count if neither of us can remember it." She hisses again. Damn that's so cute. "Will you at least turn around please? It's making me nervous having you in here." She says in a small voice that hits my heart directly.

I give her a small smile. "Sure, honey, anything that you need me to do, I will, always." I say with one hundred percent sincerity. "I promise not to look. I want you to always be comfortable around me sweetheart. Just let me know when you're covered, so that I can turn around and take a seat."

"Okay." She says in her angelic voice that would get me to do absolutely anything for her. "Thank you, Rocco."

"Anything you need to make this whole experience great for you sweetheart. Just name it and it's all yours." I leave out saying 'so am I' because I feel like that's pretty much a given at this point. Ya know, considering that I basically started telling everyone that we are together and wouldn't let her refute it.

I hear rustling behind me and it takes every single ounce of self-control that I possess to stand here and not turn around. It's really not helping my dick deflate any knowing that she's naked right behind me. How can one woman cause so much havoc to me mentally and physically and have absolutely no idea?

Whenever I pictured falling for someone and having a baby, a sweet woman with a stubborn streak a mile wide is not what I envisioned. I figured that she would be totally on board with the whole being mine thing. Nope, this stubborn ass is still trying to get out of it, even though we both know that she likes me. Let's not forget that she's already pregnant with my kid.

How the hell she's still putting up a fight is beyond me. Trust me, if she wasn't feeling the same way, she would've never kissed me back like that. And she sure as hell wouldn't have grabbed onto my hair while grinding herself on me. Why she's making both of us suffer, I'll never know. Well, that's not exactly true. I have a feeling that the fucker she dated before me put a bunch of bullshit in her head that's unfortunately stuck.

That's fine though. I have no problem showing her every step of the way how perfect I truly think that she is. Aside from her stubbornness, we could get rid of that. I chuckle mentally. Who am I kidding, even her damn stubbornness is a turn on. I might need to get my head examined if this is the type of shit that's getting me hot these days.

"Okay, you can turn around now and have a seat." Her sweet voice tells me.

I turn around and just stand there staring at the woman who will be my wife one day, even if she won't admit to it yet.

I just keep staring because this shit looks kind of weird. She's wearing a gown that looks like paper, instead of the ones they give you in the hospital and she has a big piece of paper covering her like a blanket. Aren't they supposed to make pregnant women comfortable? She looks like she's about to freeze to death.

"Are you okay?" I ask. Maybe she needs me to cover her with her clothes or something.

She frowns at me. "Yes, why?"

"You're wearing paper."

She blinks at me a few times. "This is what all women wear when they come for a gyno exam. It's for sanitary reasons."

I narrow my eyes and cross my arms. "Hospitals don't give people a thin piece of paper to wear."

"Oookkkaayyy." She's staring at me like I'm some weird experiment. How in the hell is she not mad about this?

"Aren't you the least bit upset that they have the temperature down to freezing in here and all they give you is some paper to wear? What if it fucking rips? What the hell are you supposed to do then?"

"Ask for a new one?" She answers me with a question.

I start pacing back and forth while rubbing my temples. "You wouldn't have to ask for a new one if they gave you something more substantial than this." I growl while throwing a hand out in her general direction.

She shrugs. "Maybe it's just more cost effective this way. It's probably more expensive to have it laundered than it is to purchase paper gowns in bulk." She says like the reasonable and rational adult that she is.

I stop dead in my tracks and look at her incredulously. "Shouldn't you be seeing a doctor who isn't so cheap? We want the best for you and this baby. If he's being cheap with this, what else is he being cheap with? What if he's reusing needles or something?"

She gives me a soft smile. "Rocco honey, you need to calm down. I swear that I have been coming to Dr. Piech since I first started getting my period. He is a wonderful doctor, who cares immensely about his patients. And I'm also pretty sure that it's illegal to re-use needles. Does he look like the type of man who would ever do anything illegal?"

I deflate completely and sit down. I'm sure she doesn't even realize that she called me honey. But she did. She called me honey. Ha! Finally, I'm starting to make some headway!

"I guess you're right." I reply because I didn't hear a word that she said after she called me honey. She could tell me that we're about to do some ritual sacrifice and I'd be willing to go along with it.

"Don't worry, I am." The smug ass replies.

I've definitely noticed that the more time I spend with her, the more comfortable around me she becomes. Unless I'm shirtless, but I only do that when she's frustrating the hell out of me wearing some tight ass skirt and half see-through blouse to work. I swear those little boys are some lucky fuckers and don't even realize it.

"Why are you frowning so hard and growling under your breath?" She asks with concern.

Obviously, this woman makes me brain dead because I answer without fully thinking first. "I'm thinking about all those little bastards who get to see you dressed in your hot teacher look when you wear a skirt."

I'm still mentally grumbling to myself when I realize that she hasn't said anything. I look and see her staring at me with her mouth hanging open. When she sees me looking, she closes her mouth and shakes her head.

"What in the world is wrong with you today? First you're upset over paper gowns and now you're mad that five-year-olds see me in a skirt? Are you on drugs or are you having a mental breakdown?"

"I'm a cop. Of course I'm not on drugs." I scoff.

"So, you're having a mental breakdown." She nods her head like it's a reasonable explanation.

I frown at her, leaning forward. "I'm not having a mental breakdown."

"It makes sense if you are though. Becoming a parent is a lot for people to handle when they're planning to have children. This came out of nowhere. We barely know each other and are having a baby together. That's a lot to process. And you didn't freak out when I told you. I kind of figured that it would happen at some point." She pauses to take a breath, looks around and frowns. "Though, I didn't expect it to happen at the doctor's office." She purses her luscious lips.

"I'm not having any sort of a breakdown. I'm extremely happy about this baby and who its mother is. We'll get to know each other soon enough, we have the rest of our lives for that."

She narrows her eyes at me at that statement but remains quiet. Might as well start leaving her bread crumbs to figure out that she's never getting rid of me. "I'm just incredibly upset with the level of care, or lack thereof, that you're receiving here."

"Because I'm wearing a paper gown?" She questions.

I throw my hands up in the air. She's finally getting it! "Yes!"

She nods her head. "Right, so mental breakdown it is."

I'm about to reply when we hear a few quick raps on the door before Dr. Piech walks in.

"Ah, good to see everyone is where they belong this time."

On cue, Lavender turns bright red. Damn she's too cute.

The doctor walks over to the sink and washes his hands. Good to know that he does care about somethings. He dries his hands and walks over to a big computer looking thing.

"Ready to see how far along you are and if we can get a good view of your baby?" He asks Lav as he sits on a stool in front of the computer and takes out a weird wand looking thing.

Lavender smiles sweetly at him and nods. "Yes, I've been really worried, especially since you said that this would never happen."

He tsks at her and shakes his gray haired head at her. "I said improbable, not impossible. Sometimes these things are just meant to be with the right person. Also, a stressful relationship or work can hamper fertility as well."

I'd bet my left nut that her ex asshat came here once with her and this doctor hated him just as much as everyone else seemed to. Okay, I'm liking him a little bit more, even if I think he's kind of cheap.

"I love my job, you know that." She says with a confused look on her face.

The doctor raises a bushy gray eyebrow at her and nods his head. "Yes, I do."

"Then I don't understand why I would become pregnant all of a sudden."

He stares at her with pursed lips. He looks at me with a grin and winks. "Maybe you just needed the right man."

She blushes furiously again and now I've decided that I don't give a fuck what he has her wear. He is definitely my most favorite doctor in the world.

"Anyway," He continues, "let's get this show on the road. We're going to do an internal ultrasound today to get the best picture of this little one." He looks back at me and tilts his head towards Lavender. "Dad, for the best view, why don't you go stand by Mom's head."

I smile big and stand and walk over to her. Damn that's so weird to hear the words mom and dad being used in reference to us. But fuck, if it isn't the coolest shit that I've ever heard.As I get to Lav, she gives me a bright smile that illuminates my very soul. I smile back until out of the corner of my eye I see the doctor rolling a condom over the wand thing. What the actual fuck?

He laughs, this motherfucker laughs at me when he sees the look on my face. "What's wrong?" Lav asks, as she tugs on my arm.

I look down at her with a frown. "Why is he putting a condom on that thing?"

"Because we use this on other patients, son. It's so that it remains sanitary." My eyes turn to slits. "What do you mean that you've used it on other patients?" I look down at Lav. "See, I told you that he was cheap. First the paper gowns and now this wand thing!"

Lavender places her hands in front of her face. "Oh my gosh Rocco, will you just be quiet! This is expensive equipment, of course, it would be used on more than one person." She looks at me through the gaps in her fingers. "Will you just stand there and keep your mouth shut?"

She looks over at the doctor apologetically. "I'm so sorry about him. I think that he's in the middle of a mental breakdown due to this surprise pregnancy. He's been acting like a weirdo the whole time that we've been here."

I cross my arms and glare down at her. "I have not." I mumble.

The doctor laughs and pats her arm reassuringly. "Don't worry my dear, first time fathers are always very interesting to deal with. I've gotten used to it after all these years. Now just place your legs in the stir-ups and then I'll hand you the wand to insert yourself before I take over."

Lavender starts doing as he says before what he said fully registers. "What the fuck do you mean inserted in her and you taking over?" I shout out louder than I mean to. The warning glare I receive from Lavender doesn't go unnoticed but I'm too worked up to give a damn right now.

The doctor gives me an indulgent smile, that I swear is mentally calling me a moron. "Your baby is extremely tiny at this present time." He says in a slow, patient tone. "We need this to go inside, so that we can get the best view of your baby. We need to make sure that everything is okay and that the baby is doing well."

"Oh." He raises his eyebrows at me. I cough into my hand. "Ah, continue on then."

"Gee, I'm so glad that you gave him your approval. I was so worried that we wouldn't be able to continue there for a few moments." Lavender says something straight out of Sage's playbook.

Or maybe it's a family trait that she keeps hidden. It's kind of hot. But judging by the look that she's giving me, definitely not the best time to mention it.

"Sorry sweetheart, I just want to make sure that he isn't going to do anything that hurts you." I leave out that I don't want anyone near her but me but going by both of them snorting, I have a feeling that they know my true motives.

"Can we just get this over with? Laying here like this, isn't the most comfortable thing in the whole world." Lavender says on a sigh.

After that everything goes pretty quickly and then we're looking at the computer screen. Honestly, I have no idea what we're looking at, the whole screen is dark and grainy. Then this weird sound starts and Lavender starts to cry. Shit!

"Hey doc, I think that your machine is broken. Maybe we should come back when you fix it, so that we don't upset Lav anymore."

They both start laughing and I'm not really seeing what's so funny about all of this. I look down when Lavender grabs my hand and squeezes. "It's not broken Rocco." She giggles.

I give her a look. "It obviously is. It's all dark and weird looking. Then you started crying when that weird whooshing sound started."

She starts giggling uncontrollably which I would usually find awesome, if it wasn't for the fact that I think that she's lost her mind.

"Son, she was crying happy tears." At my incredulous look he continues. "That weird whooshing sound as you put it, is your baby's heartbeat. That sound means that your baby's heart is going strong. And this grainy little image right here is your tiny little baby, safely cushioned in his or her mommy's belly."

Holy shit. That's our baby. That's the heartbeat. Holy fuck, I'm listening to my kid's heartbeat.

"You better not pass out on me right now." A tiny angelic voice tries to growl at me.

I look down and smile at Lavender. "Of course I won't." I scoff and ignore their snickers. "I was just taking a moment, that's all."

Fuck that. I will never admit to how close I was to blacking out and that I probably would if it wasn't for Lav grounding me. Jesus, this woman has more power over me than I even realized. She could break me body, mind and soul, without trying.

The rest of the visit, I spend in a sort of haze. I hear the doctor tell her that everything looks good and that she's about nine weeks along. She asks him a bunch of questions about how she was able to get pregnant in the first place. They both use a lot of terms that mean absolutely nothing to me. All I care about is the fact that my woman and my baby are fine, and they are.

He congratulates us again and tells her when to make another appointment before he leaves. I don't even get nearly as excited when I realize that she's getting naked again. What? I'm a healthy man, of course it's going to register that my woman is naked. But I was a good guy and turned around and didn't even think about peeking more than once, okay four times max, but that's it.

Once Lav is dressed, we leave the room and I trail behind her through the maze of hallways like a love-sick puppy. She gets to some window and tells them that she needs to make another appointment. The woman tells her that she doesn't need another appointment for like three months. Seriously, I thought that pregnant women went like every week or some shit?

Lavender nudges me with her arm. "Can you please pay attention?" She hisses and phrases it like a question instead of the command it truly is. "I asked you twice to take out your phone and look at your calendar to see what day works best for you. I assume that you want to come to the rest of the visits?" She challenges.

I like spunky Lavender, she's very entertaining, although I have a feeling that it's her hormones more so than her. All of my sisters became fucking nuts when they were pregnant. With Lavender usually so mild tempered, I have a feeling that she'll only get a little bit sassier. But I could be wrong and she might just turn psycho like my sisters. I really need to figure out why that excites me so much.

I look down and give her my most charming smile, hoping that it will appease her a bit. "I'm sorry honey. I was just wondering why our next appointment won't be sooner. I just want to make sure that the two of you are always okay."

"Awe." Is called by a few women on the other side of the window but we both ignore it.

I take my phone out and grab hers and sync up our calendars. "There you go, now you have my entire schedule."

She blinks at me before taking her phone back and turning around to continue scheduling her next appointment.

Me, well I just stand behind her mentally congratulating myself on being so fucking smart. I literally will know where she is every second of the day now. Fuck, I'm even better at this shit than Damon and Marc ever were.

I probably shouldn't be so proud about that. Maybe I should give JJ a call when we get out of here and see if we can stop by. I think I need to start spending more time with the only sane-ish one out of us.

I grab Lavender's hand as we're walking out of the office and she lets me. Baby steps at this point. We get to my truck and I open the door and help her in before closing it and walking around to the driver's side. I get in and buckle my seatbelt, then look over at my future wife. "Hey, do you want to stop by and see Sage and JJ?"

She chews on her bottom lip. I know that she probably wants to share today with her sister. "Yeah, I'm sure that she probably told JJ anyway. I figure that she wouldn't keep that from him."

I have a feeling that she's right since for the past couple of weeks he's been giving me curious glances. I just know that it's killing him not to say anything. Sage probably threatened his ass not to say anything.

"Plus, he probably wants to celebrate the fact that both of you will be fathers around the same time."

I was just pulling out of our parking spot when I suddenly jam on the brakes. I turn my head and look at her with wide eyes. "What did you say?"

She frowns at me. "Didn't I tell you?" I shake my head slowly and she casually shrugs. "Yes, well apparently, we weren't the only irresponsible ones during the trip to Vegas."

"Didn't he get a vasectomy?" I know that he did, because we all had a shit load of fun making fun of him.

Lavender does the cutest little pig snort. "Yup, but by then it was already too late." She starts giggling and doesn't stop until we're halfway to their house.

Not that I mind. Her giggle definitely soothes something in me that I didn't even realize needed soothing.

She wipes at her eyes. "Oh my gosh, only my sister would get pregnant right before her husband gets fixed." She giggles again. "I swear, she has the world's worst luck when it comes to getting knocked up." She chuckles.

I look at her from the corner of my eye while I continue driving. "Have you said that to her?"

"Are you crazy? She's mean and would punch me in the boob. Trust me, that hurts a lot more than you think that it would. She's such an evil witch sometimes."

"You women are so strange." I mumble a lot louder than I meant to.

"What was that?" She asks in that tone, that tone that every man knows and dreads. That tone that says you fucked up and this isn't going to be a pleasant few minutes.

"Ah. What honey?" Deflect whenever possible or just act dumb. Acting dumb has saved my ass plenty of times over the years. Hopefully that tradition holds up.

She sucks on her teeth for a second while looking at me like she's sucking on a lemon. I forgot those damn hormones come out of nowhere. "I thought that you had called me strange...that's all." Her voice is way too high-pitched and chipper right now.

"Definitely not baby. You're the most perfect woman ever. I could never think that the mother of my unborn child was strange." The slip up is going to cost me so I start thinking of ways to make up for it. A brownie maybe?

"Right." She says while side-eyeing me with her arms crossed against her chest. I ignore the clicking of her tongue. Nothing good will come from me engaging her right now. I've been in enough battles to know when to fucking retreat.

I see the grocery store up ahead and it's like God is looking out for me. Like I'm getting a chance to fix this, or at least get away from the angry, hormonal pregnant one for a few minutes.

"Hey sweetheart?" I ignore her glare filled raised eyebrow. "Would you like me to stop at the store and pick up some ice cream and brownies for you and Sage? Those were always favorites for my sisters when they were pregnant."

"I guess." She says with only a little hiss, that makes me pleased with the little progress.

"Any particular flavor of ice cream, or should I just get a few? That way you guys can pick and choose later?" I ask calmly like I'm in no way shape or form fearing for my safety right now.

"Having a few options would probably be a good idea. I don't know what Sage will want right now."

I pull into the parking lot of the grocery store, at only a slightly high speed. I also may or may not have cut someone off to make sure that I made the turn. That person can kiss my ass though. They're not currently dealing with a pissed off pregnant woman.

I look over and see Lavender glaring at me while white knuckling the side of the door. Her glare is also back in full force. "Are you crazy? You just cut that old man off."

"Not really. He's like ninety and driving close to ten under the speed limit. I had plenty of time. I'm a cop remember. I'm good at judging these things."

I park the truck and unbuckle my seatbelt. I look at her and give her my little boy smile that tends to even get me out of shit with my sisters.

"Is there anything else that you want sweetheart?" She shakes her head no. "Okay, I'll be right back then." I say with a hell of a lot of false enthusiasm that Lavender narrows her eyes at.

I close the door and if I happen to walk more briskly than usual, then so be it.

Sage opens the door and raises her eyebrow at the two of us on her doorstep. Luckily, she doesn't voice any of the obvious questions running through her mind. She opens the door wide and waves her arm in an arc to allow us to enter.

I hold up the only bag that Rocco let me carry – the brownies since they're light – and give my sister a somewhat unforced smile. "We brought ice cream and brownies." Her eyes light up and she turns on her heel and starts walking towards the kitchen without uttering one word.

JJ comes walking down the hall as Sage passes him without a glance. He tilts his head and then looks in our direction with a smile. "Hey guys. What's going on?"

I smile back at my new brother-in-law. "I told Sage that we brought brownies and ice cream and she's decided to be rude and just haul butt into the kitchen."

"I'm getting us bowls and spoons bitch! I've known you all my life, saying hello is totally unnecessary when brownies are involved." We all hear shouted from the kitchen.

JJ just shakes his head and looks at the bags in our hands. He gives Rocco a head nod towards the kitchen. "You better bring her those bags before she comes out here and guts you for them."

I hold out my hand for Rocco to hand me the other bags so that I can join my sister in the kitchen. He looks down at my hand like I'm crazy. "Why are you sticking your hand out?" The man who is now just annoying me asks. Good to know that if he's annoying, I won't focus on how gorgeous he is and get tongue tied.

"I'm holding out my hand so that you'll give me the other bags, so that I can go join my sister in the kitchen." I explain patiently like I'm talking to one of the children at work.

"I'll bring everything in. No need for you to carry anything heavy." Awesome, here we go again.

"Rocco, for the fourth time in the last ten-minutes, I am more than capable of carrying a few bags filled with ice cream containers."

His eyes narrow slightly. "Yes, I'm sure that you can. But why should you have to if I'm around and more than willing to do it?"

I narrow mine right back at the annoying, sweet Adonis standing in front of me. "Because it doesn't make sense for you to carry it into the kitchen when I'm already going in there. It makes sense to just hand me the darn bags Rocco."

JJ is being absolutely no help what-so-ever. He's leaning against the wall with his arms crossed against his chest. One leg is crossed against the other and he has a smirk on his face. The three girls come walking down the hall and stop to stare at all of us.

"Hey aunt Lav, what's going on?" Missy asks while the other two look on with rapt attention.

I look over and smile at the girls. It's not their fault Rocco is pushing my patience to the limit. "I'm just trying to explain to Rocco, that I am more than capable of carrying a few bags into the kitchen." I say through only slightly gritted teeth.

Becca walks forward with a curious look on her face. Lord help me now. Nothing that ever comes out of her mouth is ever appropriate.

She tilts her head at me with an evil little grin. "Is it because you're a woman or because you're all preggers and baby daddy is going all caveman?"

"Sage!" I yell with my hands on my hips.

"It's not my fault that they have freakish Vulcan hearing." She yells back from the kitchen.

"Actually, we don't." Missy states blandly. "The older you get, the louder you talk. We didn't even have to try to listen in on that conversation."

Paige looks at JJ with a similar evil grin to Becca's. "You both should really get your hearing checked. Because neither of you talk quietly. We hear every conversation that you two have. Hearing aids might not be a bad idea for you guys."

JJ narrows his eyes at the three. "Don't you have some evil to go and do somewhere or an animal sacrifice to make. Anywhere that isn't here?"

We hear a horn beep three times in rapid succession. "Saved by the horn." Becca chirps. "Dad's taking us for the night to some training thing. So please try to get all your gross sex stuff out of the way while we're gone." The other two nod their heads in agreement.

"I swear, I'm beginning to love your father more than I love you three each day that passes."

"I feel like that's something that you might need to discuss with Mom. Did getting neutered, after knocking Mom up with the most likely demon child, turn you gay? Mom's hormonal right now and would be upset if her husband was in love with her original baby daddy." Becca says.

JJ pinches the bridge of his nose as I can feel Rocco at my back shaking with laughter. "You really wonder why the other two are our favorites?"

She shrugs casually. "I'm Dad's favorite, so it makes sense that someone else likes these two." She tosses a thumb over her shoulder at the two girls at her back.

"We love you girls! Have fun with your dad! Don't come back until tomorrow night preferably!" Sage yells from the kitchen.

"What she said." JJ says as he starts pushing – ushering – the girls out the door. With a wave to Danny he shoves them out and slams the door.

He looks at us. "You'll understand one day. Trust me, you can love them from afar." He gives us a huge dimple filled smile. "So, I finally get to say congratulations."

"Apparently, since you two talk so loud." Rocco drawls with a happy lilt in his voice.

The guys do that whole weird bro-hug thing. You know, where they half hug each other and half slap each other a lot. I never understood why men can't just be normal and hug like you're supposed to.

JJ comes over to me and literally picks me up in a gigantic bear hug and actually spins me around. "Whoa, will you put her down and be careful. Jesus man, don't spin her around like that." Rocco says in a near panic.

JJ and I both look at Rocco who looks like he's on the verge of a meltdown. We then look at each other and start laughing.

We ignore the crazy one who is still huffing and puffing about it being bad for him to be picking me up like this. I swear, I might have Damon and Declan hide Rocco somewhere until after this pregnancy is over. We're only nine weeks in and he's already this bad. For his own safety, they might need to place him somewhere far away from me.

JJ finally puts me down when we're done laughing at Rocco. Rocco practically pushes JJ out of his way and looks me over from head to toe. I really never would've guessed that he was such a crazy person.

I swat at his hands that are running all over my body, much to my hormones dismay. "Will you cut it out. I'm absolutely fine Rocco. Geez, you haven't been this bad before. Knock it off, it was just a hug."

He stands in front of me with his arms crossed, eyes narrowed and feet apart. Good grief, he acts like he's gearing up for battle. I hear JJ snort and walk out of the room while muttering "Good luck" though I'm not really sure which one of us he's talking to.

"All of that hugging and spinning could've hurt the baby. What if he squeezed too hard or spun you around too much? There's a reason that they don't let pregnant women go on rides in amusement parks."

I blink at him a few times and then blink some more. "You just compared a hug to a rollercoaster ride. Do you understand how insane you sound right now?"

"I obviously meant it figuratively." I'm sure he did, I snigger to myself. "But really what if it hurt the baby in some way? You should be resting as much as possible so that nothing happens to you or the baby."

And I'm back to blinking. He has three sisters, who have all been pregnant and given birth. There is no way that he can be this crazy about it. Absolutely not. I know two of his sisters. They would've killed him if he acted like this with them.

"Rocco," I start in a gentle tone. Maybe if I talk softly, he'll calm down a bit, "pregnant women are able to do almost everything that non-pregnant ones can do. I mean, most women even work right up until a few weeks or even a few days before giving birth."

"What are you talking about? You're not going back to work. What if one of the kids gets you sick or bumps into your stomach and harms the baby? Oh no, definitely not. You need to put in for that leave thing right away. We can't take any chances." He finishes his crazy little rant while pacing back and forth and pulling on his hair.

Oh my gosh! This incredibly gorgeous and incredibly sexy man is certifiably insane! It makes complete sense why he's been fixated on me...he's nuts! That explains everything! I only seem to attract either mean or crazy men. I should've known. And great, I'm having his baby and stuck with his crazy butt for the next eighteen years.

He stops pacing and stares at me with a frown. "Why are you looking at me like that?"

"Like what?" I question with a head tilt. I'm curious as to what my face looks like since I have so many thoughts running through my head at the present moment.

"Like I kicked your puppy but you were expecting me to. It's a weird look that's making me kind of uneasy right now."

"Well, all of this makes sense to me now." I tell him.

"What makes sense?" He asks dubiously.

"You and I." I ignore his smile. "You're obviously a crazy person. And since I only seem to attract men that are either mean or crazy, all of this makes complete sense now. I knew that you were probably too good to be true. I actually feel better knowing that my life is still on its usual course and not totally spinning off of its axis."

"Sage and JJ get in here please." He hollers.

I cross my arms and start tapping my foot. "I don't see what they have to do with this."

He holds up a hand for me to stop talking as we wait for Sage and JJ to come back in. Of course, my sister who only thinks with her stomach, grabs all of the bags from our hands while mumbling "I'll put these in the fridge," and walking back into the kitchen.

"Am I crazy or insane?" Rocco asks JJ.

JJ gives us both a smirk. "Normally no, but impending fatherhood doesn't seem to be agreeing with you at the moment. You just told your woman not to go back to work in case a kid bumps into her. Even you have to see how ridiculous you're being right now."

"I'm not his woman." I interject and am completely ignored. How lovely.

"Okay fine, I guess that was a bit much. But she's walking around acting like it's no big deal."

"She's standing right here and can hear you." I mutter more to myself, since no one else seems to listen to me.

Sage walks in eating the rest of what looks to have been a brownie. "Rocco, you need to understand that women have babies all the time. Our bodies are literally made for this. She'll be fine and you need to calm the hell down before she asks someone to shank you." She says after having swallowed a rather large piece of brownie.

I turn towards her with a frown. Mine almost matching the one that Rocco is wearing, not that I notice or anything. "You spend way too much time with Kayla. Who actually talks about shanking someone?"

She turns and points a brownie covered finger at me. Geez, how many did she scarf down before she came back in here? "And you!"

She shouts way too loudly for someone standing so close. Maybe the girls are right and she is going deaf.

"You need to stop telling people that he isn't your man. Face facts, you're both together, whether you've been wanting to admit it to yourself or not. He's not just going to spend every spare moment that he has with someone he doesn't want to." She takes a deep breath and looks at us. "You're probably driving him this crazy because you keep refuting what everyone else sees. That you two are together and adorable. Now get your shit together. Because you two are about to have a baby and the last thing you two need to be bickering about is whether or not you're in a relationship that everyone already knows that you're in."

"I never agreed to be in a relationship. This crazy man," I wave an arm in Rocco's direction "took it upon himself to start telling everyone that we were in one. It would've been nice to have had a choice in the matter." I huff.

Sage gives me a bland look and shrugs. "You over think things too much. Honestly, if he had given you time to think, you would've found a way to chicken out of the whole relationship. This way, everyone already thinks that you're in one, so it takes all the pressure and thinking away."

My eyes narrow into tiny slits. "Did you have something to do with him announcing to everyone that we're together?" I hiss out.

She rolls her eyes at me. "Duh." She snorts like an evil overweight pig. "If I hadn't, that love-sick dope would've given you way too much time to come up with an exit strategy. Now you can't."

"When we're done being pregnant, I'm going to murder you. I'm stuck with him now."

"Damn sweetheart, you just really know how to raise a man's ego up." Rocco drawls at me.

I turn and point an index finger at him. "I don't want to hear a peep out of you mister. You went right along with her crazy plan."

He scoffs at me and ignores my warning glare. "Of course I did. I wanted you more than my next breath. You were pretending that I didn't exist or whatever it was that you were doing. Sage came up with a plan and I went with it."

Okay, I won't lie, I may have swooned internally a tiny little bit at the "wanting you more than my next breath" part but still. "You both are completely insane!" I screech with wide eyes.

Sage snickers. "The only one acting crazy right now is you." She looks over at Rocco for a moment. "Well, except for him losing it over a hug and working with kids. But I still feel like you're probably to blame for his lack of mental stability these days."

"Thanks...I think?" Rocco sort of states.

Sage claps her hands. "Now, let's go have some ice cream and brownies. We can decide all the important stuff like where you're going to live and stuff while stuffing our faces."

"What are you talking about? We both have our own homes and who said anything about changing where either of us lives?" I ask in horror.

"Actually, I only have an apartment and my lease is almost up anyway. I figured that we would just stay in your house for now." Rocco states calmly, effectively freaking me out even further.

"Who said anything about us living together?"

"It's the natural progression of a relationship Lav." My soon-to-be-dead-to-me sister states. "Sure, you guys are bumping it up a bit, but I mean you are together and pregnant. Might as well move in together to make everything easier." She shrugs casually, like this isn't a massive decision.

I wave my hands around. "Hello. Earth to crazy people. I still have not agreed to even be in this relationship, nor have I agreed to let anyone move in with me. How are you guys actually not seeing that this is an entirely insane plan?" I look over at JJ with pleading eyes. Someone in this group has to be sane. "JJ, a little help please? You know this is crazy."

He gives me a sheepish look and rubs the back of his head. "Lav, you know that I adore you. But there is no way in hell that I am going up against my pregnant wife and one of my best friends. I'm sorry sweet girl, but you are on your own."

"You are all insane. There is absolutely no way in hades that I am going to agree to any of this crazy nonsense!" I shout with my arms firmly crossed. There is no way that I am going to allow any of this happen.

Three Weeks Later:

"Where do you guys want this last box?" Declan asks in an annoyingly chipper voice.

I still cannot believe that I have somehow been sideswiped again in my own life. This is honesty beginning to get a bit ridiculous that everyone refuses to listen to me.

"Back at his own apartment, where it belongs." I answer sweetly.

I hear Damon cough and it suspiciously sounds like a laugh. Declan just ignores me and continues to place all of Rocco's belongings in my house. My now very crowded house.

I'm sitting on my couch in what was once a very quiet and peaceful living room. Now, it's crowded, loud and filled with men helping their buddy move in. This would be fine if I had agreed to any of this, alas, I did not. So, to say that I'm a bit cranky is an understatement.

At least all of the men have been smart enough to keep their distance. Except for Declan, who has been all up in my personal space today. I'm not sure who he is trying to annoy more, me or Rocco, but it seems to be working equally well, so bravo to him.

I can hear myself starting to sound like Sage with all of these snarky thoughts. I swear, ever since I became pregnant, I just cannot get a handle of any of my emotions. I go from happy and carefree one moment, to hysterically crying because they were out of my favorite chocolate covered pretzels at the store. I'm constantly on an emotional rollercoaster that I do not want to be on.

Add in the gorgeous but soon to be maimed Adonis that has steamrolled his way into my life and you could say that I've been a tiny bit crabby. I know for a fact that the man in question is not deaf nor is he dumb.

Yet somehow all of my protests to this ridiculous idea have gone unheard. Anytime I manage to corner him and ask him why he's doing all of this he plays dumb and acts like it's news to him that I am not on board with any of this.

A pregnant woman can only take so much before she snaps. And I know that I should be over the moon to have the man that I've had the world's biggest crush on – for longer than I shall ever make known – actually want to be with me and move in. But I've learned in life, that if something seems too good to be true, it usually is. I'm not a cynic by any stretch but after my relationship with Derrick, well let's just say that I'm weary. Would I love for all of this to be true and have Rocco fall madly and deeply in love with me? Sure. That's every girl's dream from the time she watches her first Disney movie and wants to marry the prince. But this is real life and sometimes – most of the time – the prince is actually a frog with a lot of warts.

I knew I sounded cynical but fairytales didn't come true. Any they definitely didn't start with a drunken night in Vegas and a surprise – never an accident – baby. Worse still, is now that I'm at the thirteen-week mark, Rocco wants to start telling everyone. I could still stay in my bubble before everyone knew. That won't be possible afterwards. Okay, I'm really just a coward, but I'm blaming it all on the hormones, might as well be useful for something.

I look down and see what has unceremoniously landed in my lap and look up to see who threw it, as Sage plops down next to me.

"Here, have a Snickers, maybe it will make the resting bitch face you have going on...go away." My oh so lovely sister taunts.

I give her a nasty look but proceed to open the candy bar. No need to waste good candy just because I want to throw it at her right now. I'll save broccoli for throwing.

"You're too kind." I mumble around the mouth full of candy.

"You're so classy." Sage sighs as she tries to get comfortable. "No wonder you were able to snag Rocco so easily." She pretends to be in awe.

If I wasn't so hungry, the rest of this candy bar would be all over her right now. "I didn't snag him. You helped him insert himself into my life without my approval."

She curls up on her left side and leans her arm against the back of the couch. "See, that's what I don't get. You like him, anyone with eyes can see that. Yet, you've been fighting this tooth and nail. The man literally can't say that he's anymore committed to you. He's moving himself in for you for fuck's sake!" She whisper hisses at me.

I tilt my head and look her directly in the eyes. "And if I wasn't pregnant? Where do you think he would be then?"

She stares at me for a few beats without blinking. She shakes her head, almost as if she's dislodging something. "That's why you've been fighting this the whole time?" She asks me with an incredulous tone in her voice.

I don't see why she's so surprised. I think it's a very logical way to look at this. "It's really not that much of a stretch of the imagination sis. He hasn't left me alone since finding out that I was pregnant. It stands to reason, that because he is a stand-up guy, that he would try to make this work between us for the baby's sake." I tell her rationally. In all honesty, it's what makes the most sense.

"Has it ever occurred to you that this way was the only way to actually become a part of your life?" She purses her lips like she's sucking on a lemon.

"What do you mean?"

She rolls her eyes and acts all put out like I'm an idiot. "That man has been trying to get your attention for months...months!" She hisses like a snake again. "You've pretty much ignored him."

"You know why." I try to defend.

She nods her head a bit. "Yes, you were definitely very spastic around him in the beginning, trust me, no one who saw you near him will ever argue that fact. I think he's the only one who didn't realize why you were pretending to ignore him. And that's probably only because it frustrated him so much. But Lav, even you have to see that he's liked you for a long time. He saw this as his way to finally be a part of your life and he held onto it with both hands. Why do you think everyone is helping him without even knowing that your pregnant?" She snorts. "Shit, if they all knew about you being preggers, they would've moved his ass in weeks ago girl."

"It's just hard to trust something that seems a little too good to be true, you know? Like, why would a man who looks like him and is as kind as he is, want an awkward and boring school teacher? You've seen the type of women who throw themselves at him. Those are the types of women that he should be with. Not plain Janes like me." I finish on a sigh.

She's shaking her head angrily at me. "I swear, next time I see Derrick, I'm finding a way to run his ass over with my car." She mutters but continues before I can say anything. "Lav, you have to know everything that you just said is a huge bunch of bullshit girl. You're beyond gorgeous with curves for days. Trust me, your brain did not factor into his initial lust." She chuckles. "And has it ever occurred to you that he likes the whole teacher thing? He has been trying to get your attention there for months. Cut the guy some slack already...will ya?"

I shrug. "We'll see."

"Poor Rocco." She says with pity.

My eyes widen. "Poor Rocco?" I sputter. "I'm the one whose house and body has been invaded. If you're feeling sorry for anyone, it should be me."

"Nu-huh." She shakes her head. "Not only has that guy already put in months and months-worth of work, but he still has a long ass uphill battle ahead of him with you. If anything, it just makes me want to go out and buy the poor man a case of beer and wish him luck." She tells me and then mutters. "He's going to need it."

"You are absolutely no help what-so-ever." I huff and play with the wrapper from the candy bar. I wonder if she has any more stashed on her anywhere?

She blinks a few times and gives me an evil smile. "Kay said the same thing to me not too long ago. I don't know why you two assume that I'm trying to help you at all."

"Probably because you're my sister and her best friend." I deadpan.

She shrugs one shoulder carelessly. "Eh, I'm just here for the entertainment. Plus, you've been super bitchy lately and it's been a lot of fun to watch. You're the Lavender that I always knew you could be."

I squint my eyes and give her my own version of an evil grin. "I always figured that you were a big enough witch for the both of us."

"And there goes all of my pride in you. Would it kill you to actually curse?" She whines like one of my students.

"Would it kill you not to be so crass all of the time?"

She pulls out two more candy bars from seemingly thin air and hands me one. "Touché bitch, touché."

She nods her head and we both sit quietly eating our candy bars while ignoring that my life is turning into a weird sitcom. Denial is a wonderful thing at times. I sigh silently to myself.

I'm sitting outside in the backyard at Lavender's, well I guess now my house, and look at the other men sitting with me. I really did luck out with having such a great group of friends. Who else would ignore the protests of the woman whose house they were moving stuff into? Not fully functional and mentally stable people...that's for sure. I tilt my head down. Jesus, we're all going to hell, every single one of us.

I look up in time to see the beer that JJ is handing me. I grab it and pop the top off, before taking a long pull. I look around at all the guys and ask the question that's been running through my mind the most today. "What do you think the chances of her stabbing me in my sleep are?"

"Does she realize that you're not sleeping on the couch?" Morris asks and I shake my head no.

Declan looks at me and shrugs. "Just sleep lightly. Normal Lav definitely wouldn't. Pregnant and hormonal Lav, well she's been a fun little wildcard lately."

At his statement every man, other than JJ, stops and stares at him and then me.

Marc blinks a few times before tilting his head. "Is it yours?" I nod, not entirely offended considering I forced my way into her life. "How did you knock her up when she won't let you anywhere near her?"

I'm momentarily brought back to my hazy memories of that night.

"Yeah, I've actually been wondering about that since I figured out that she was pregnant." Declan states.

Marc raises a beer filled hand at him. "We'll get back to how your dumbass figured out that she was pregnant before the rest of us in just a minute. But my question first."

That's actually a pretty good question, he still doesn't realize that he's been hitting on a lesbian for years but figures out that Lav is pregnant. That shit just doesn't make any sense, but I answer Marc first. "Vegas."

All of them nod like that makes sense. "Those tequila shots did you both some good, huh?" Damon chuckles.

I grimace. "Well good for me in a way, since I finally have the woman of my dreams. Bad because I'm pretty sure that she's going to stab me to death at some point."

"No, Lavender is too sweet. She'll just maim you a bit." Morris supplies unhelpfully.

"That makes me feel so much better." I drawl.

"It should." Marc nods his head. "At least that way, you'll get to meet your kid. You may end up looking like *Freddy Kreuger* or some shit, but at least this kid will be cute."

"He's got a point." Damon agrees.

I look over at JJ with a droll look. "Remind me again why you approved all of their applications?"

He smiles evilly. "They were the only ones who applied. I didn't have any other options."

"Haha, you two are sooooo funny." Declan deadpans.

Marc looks over at him. "Anyway, back to you, our village idiot, how did you figure out that Lav was pregnant?"

Declan's almost mastered Damon's bland serial killer look, especially while looking at Marc, I muse happily.

Declan looks around and shrugs. "It was pretty obvious." At everyone's raised eyebrows he just rolls his eyes and takes a swig of his beer.

"Seriously, anyone who's ever spent any time with her knows that she's an absolute sweetheart. So, her being grumpy once, sure, maybe it was that time of the month. Her being able to give Sage and Kayla a run for their money for weeks now? Nope, no fucking way. The only thing that made sense was that she either became a bitch overnight, which is unlikely since she still won't curse properly, or she was knocked up."

He looks over at me with a bright smile. "I'm just really glad to know that it's yours buddy. And a little disappointed."

"Why in the hell would you be disappointed?" JJ asks him before I can.

He sniffs a little, actually motherfucking sniffs. "It would've been nice to have some fun and someone new to mess with. And if her baby daddy had happened to have an accident" - he shrugs casually – "well, I mean those things happen."

Marc and Damon nod along with him, while I'm sure that I have the same horrified look on my face that Morris and JJ do. We have got to be the most fucked up team on the planet.

"I don't know whether to be worried that you would want to get rid of her baby daddy for me or touched." I scratch the side of my head with the hand that isn't holding the beer. Beer that I am going to need a lot more of after this conversation.

"Anything for you buddy." He says while giving me a smile that's only slightly creepy.

"Thanks...I think."

"Don't encourage him." JJ mumbles to me.

I look over at him with wide eyes. "Those three encourage each other. No one else has anything to do with it. They're nightmares all on their own." I tell him.

"I was somewhat offended until the nightmares part. I kind of like that one. It feels right." Marc says seriously while Damon grunts his agreement and Declan just nods his head.

"The three of you really see nothing wrong with that?" Morris questions while holding onto his beer like it has the meaning of life in it.

Marc turns his head and gives Morris a glare. "Don't act all high and mighty, like you've never helped us out."

Morris glares back at him annoyed that they've decided to have a pissing match right now. "The only reason I helped is because Michelle's ex was a verbally abusive asshole. You know damn well that's the only reason I helped cover for you guys when he got hit by that car."

"I still think that, that was an act of God. Or just Karma for him being such a huge douchebag." Marc says merrily.

Okay, I can't say that I was overly sorry to hear that he had run into the street and gotten hit by that car. Truthfully, it did seem like Karma was working some of her magic right then. Hmmmm.

"Lavender has a really shitty ex." I tell them.

JJ and Morris give me warning looks, while the other three are looking at me like I just gave their lives meaning. I'm probably going to regret ever saying that. I snort mentally. No I won't. Well, not if those three can get away with whatever they come up with perfectly.

JJ looks over at me with a scowl on his face. "What happened to, 'I don't encourage them'?" He asks me through gritted teeth.

I give him the same smile that I give my mom whenever she looks like she's pissed at me. Judging by the look on his face, it works a lot better on her. "My bad."

He blinks and just chugs the rest of his beer.

Several Hours Later:

I'm in the kitchen cleaning up all the beer bottles and pizza boxes left over from today. One of the conditions of the guys helping me today, was that I supply them with pizza and beer. I would've supplied them with anything if it helped get me closer to my end goal with Lavender.

Speaking of my wonderful, pregnant, pissed off woman who shoots daggers at me every time our eyes meet. "I still can't believe that you actually did this." She says with her arms folded over her chest while tapping a slipper covered foot.

She looks so fucking adorable with her hair up in a messy bun, unicorn pajamas and matching unicorn slippers. It's almost like she's trying her hardest to make herself unappealing. Too bad this side of her is more appealing than any woman that I have ever seen out at the bar. The fact that she's like a pissed off kitten right now is like the icing on the cake.

Jesus, I'm beginning to think that I have some weird ass fetishes. Or this woman has thrown me for a complete mind fuck. I was completely normal until I met her.

"Did what, sweetheart?" I blink innocently. Playing dumb has been working out pretty well for the past couple of weeks.

"Don't start playing dumb with me Rocco Anthony!" I'm sure it was one of my traitorous sisters who revealed my name to her. "We both know darn well that you know exactly what I'm talking about."

She takes a seat at the island and leans both arms on the top like she's gearing up to fight for a while.

"What do you want me to say Lav?" I hold my arms out at my sides. "That I've wanted you for months and that ignoring all of your protests was the only way to get anywhere with your stubborn ass?" The words come out a bit louder than I intended but it's been a long couple of months since the big announcement and I'm growing frustrated.

She blinks at me a few times and then sighs long and loudly. "Rocco let's be realistic here for a few minutes...okay?"

Instead of grabbing the beer bottle that I really, really want to grab, I grab two bottles of water and hand one to Lav, and keep the other for myself.

"Thank you." She says sweetly as she takes the bottle.

I tilt my head side to side a few times until it cracks on both sides. "Okay, I'm ready now. What's up sweetheart?"

She starts giggling and shaking her head at me. "You're nuts." She giggles angelically again. I could listen to her do that forever. "It's not like you're about to get in the ring with Mike Tyson."

I nod seriously. "Maybe not but I still have a feeling that it is going to be a big uphill battle."

"What is with you and Sage?" She mutters to what I'm assuming is herself before continuing. "I just think that we shouldn't try to make a relationship between us work just for the baby's sake."

I blink and then blink some more. Either this woman is deaf, dumb and blind and I know that she's not, or that shithead ex really did a number on her. I would bet everything I own that it was her ex. She has to have seen me trying – and failing miserably – to get her attention every time I was within a hundred feet of her.

I take a deep breath and try to calm myself down. It will only work against me if I get upset with her.

"Lavender," I use her full name, hoping that she grasps how utterly serious I am right now, "you can't seriously believe that's the only reason that I've done all of this?" I point towards the unpacked boxes.

She gives me an uncertain look and starts chewing on her bottom lip. I can't believe that she actually believes that bullshit!

Keep it together I tell myself breathing deeply through my nose. I try to relax.

"So, let me get this straight." I try to say as evenly and as casually as possible. "You really do believe that bullshit? That I'm just here because of the baby?"

Her eyelids lower a smidge. "It's not bullcrap Rocco. It's very reasonable for me to believe that's why you've gone through so much trouble." She huffs with annoyance evident in her voice. Right, because she's the one who should be annoyed right now.

I look her right in the eyes. "What about all of those times at the school that I would try to talk to you and you would walk away as fast as possible after making sure that Ella was safe with me?"

"Ah...." She trails off.

"What about all of those times that I would try to start up a conversation with you, when we were out with everyone? Only to have you ignore my very existence and talk to everyone else but me?"

She holds up an index finger. "See, I can explain that." She somewhat stutters. If I wasn't so worked up, I would care more about the fact that her face is turning redder and redder. But I just don't have it in me right now.

"What about every single phone call, text message and voicemail that I left? For weeks **before** I found out that you were pregnant?" I say through gritted teeth.

Unable to sit still I start pacing back and forth. I mean seriously, how can this woman not get the fact that it's her, in all of her awful stubbornness, that I fucking want?

"Guys like you don't date women like me, not forever anyway." She whispers so lowly that I almost miss it with my pacing and racing thoughts, but I don't.

I stop dead in my tracks and turn my head to look at her. She has her head down and her hands in her lap. When she looks up at me with unshed tears in her eyes, every ounce of anger evaporates immediately. Shit, she really believes that.

How can this woman not see how incredible she is? Christ, I mean every kid within a mile radius has to hug her a million times before they leave. The mothers hang onto every word she says like she's some weird angelic prophet. The fathers...well some of those fuckers need to chill. Most of those bastards are married and need to stop staring at her ass like they're going to get a piece. Because they sure as hell aren't!

"Why are you growling?" Lavender asks me with a dubious look on her face.

I blink a few times. "What are you talking about, sweetheart?" I frown.

She leans away from me a little bit. "You just stopped, sort of got a dazed look and then an angry one. After that your eyes got all squinty and you started growling. Are you drunk or having delusions that you're some sort of animal?"

"No."

"No to what?" She purses those luscious lips.

I shrug. "All of it. I was just having an unpleasant thought that's never, ever going to happen."

"Right." She's now side-eyeing me like I'm some sort of werewolf wannabe freak.

"Anyway," I say to get us back on track and off of why I suddenly have started to growl. I'm seriously losing it these days, "about all of that shit that you just said."

She huffs and squints her eyes at me but remains silent.

"Why would you ever think something like that Lav? You have to know that you're fucking gorgeous." I enjoy the blush that comes over her face quite a bit. "I tried for months to get your attention, sweetheart, and you ignored me at every turn."

"I didn't actually ignore you." She mumbles bashfully looking down at her lap and twisting her fingers again.

"Then what were you doing, because honestly Lav, it sucked balls...big time."

Still looking down at her lap she rushes out the most wonderful little rant that I've ever heard, well besides the rant where she told me that I was going to be a dad.

"I couldn't talk to you. Literally, every time that I would try, my brain would stop working and it would just go blank. So, the few times that I was actually going to try I would just sputter randomly." Pausing she looks around unsure before continuing "When we were out with everyone, they all seemed to figure out that I just couldn't talk to you. So, they took pity on me and helped me by engaging me in conversations."

It's really hard for me to grasp the words that are coming out of her mouth but I try.

"You have no idea what it's like for a guy who looks like every woman's fantasy to give you their sole attention. It's absolutely nerve-racking. Add in the fact that I've liked you for so long and, well, yeah it kind of just made everything worse."

She finishes and takes a huge gulp of air. Okay, so I learned a few things from this rant. One, all of my friends are assholes who knew damn well that I would've given my left foot to get her to talk to me and still helped her ignore me.

Two, I obviously make her very uncomfortable, which is not a good thing when trying to start a relationship with the woman who owns you without realizing it.

And three, thank fuck, she does like me! And she seems to think that I look like every woman's fantasy. Not that I actually give a fuck about that, but as long as I'm her fantasy, I'm a very happy man.

"So, I'm your fantasy man huh?" I say and can feel the cheesy ass grin on my face.

"That's all that you got out of everything that I just said?" She asks me with wide eyes.

I shake my head no. "I heard everything that you said, and trust me, we'll be going over a lot of it at a later time. But as long as I finally know that you like me, I'm a happy man."

"I obviously like you, you big dope!" She yells and throws her arms up in the air. "I had sex with you and I'm now carrying your baby. If that doesn't say that I like you, I don't know what does."

"Yeah, but we were both drunk. Hell, both of us barely remember much of that night." Okay, this is the moment that all the little baby steps of progress that I had just made recently, disappeared.

There are some moments in life where you realize after it's way too late that you should've never opened your mouth. The second that I said that, I knew, just knew that I had fucked up. I really only have myself to blame for the glare that is currently being shot in my direction.

"You think that I would just sleep with any random person because I was drunk?" She asks incredulously.

"That it wouldn't matter to me who I went off with and spent the night with? Do you think that I would be remotely comfortable enough to get drunk with someone that I didn't like and trust to some degree?" Her tone has gone from loud to soft and low now, almost lethal.

"That's not how I meant it at all Lav!" I try to back track as fast as possible, even though I already know that the damage is done. "I was just saying that the whole night is hazy. I didn't mean anything by it."

She gives me a creepy smile that a woman who's plotting your death gives you. "Oh, so you didn't mean that you think that I'm a whore for getting drunk and having sex with you? That's so great to know! Makes me feel just so awesome." She chirps.

Honestly, I'm too scared to even move at this point. A pissed off woman is one thing. A pissed off pregnant woman is a whole different battle. I'm afraid to even breathe too loudly with the icy glare that I'm currently on the receiving end of.

"I trust that you can figure out where the blankets and pillows are stored. The couch is very comfortable. Have a wonderful evening Rocco. Sleep well." She says with her head raised and ice in her voice. Any warmth that I had felt is gone and in its place is a frozen tundra of pissed off woman.

I do the only smart thing I can do, which is nod my head and watch her calmly walk out of the room. The only warmth is the steam that I can practically see rising from her head. Well, there goes any thoughts of cuddling up to my pregnant woman. I probably should sleep lightly...for a while.

I normally love Mondays. I know, I know, I'm some weird freak of nature. But I absolutely love my job. There is nothing better than seeing all twenty-six of my students come in super excited to tell me everything that they did over the weekend.

A child's excitement just can't be matched. And their happiness has always made me happy. Well, except for this Monday. I shouldn't really say that, I'm still happy, just a little grumpy. But I blame that more on a certain annoying and handsome man than anything else.

Well that and the fact that I haven't had a good night's sleep since he moved himself in two nights ago. You would think that I would sleep better with him in the house. But between the lack of sleep and raging hormones I am starting to feel as if I am turning into some sex crazed teenager or worse, my parents.

Seeing him walk around in gray sweats with his abs showing had me checking to make sure I wasn't literally drooling. I know that he's got to be doing it on purpose. Who in their right mind would cook bacon shirtless? That's just asking for a trip to the hospital. I'll admit, the man can cook though, it was some of the best bacon that I've ever had in my entire life.

A hand being waved in front of me brings me out of my daze and causes me to jump back in my chair a smidgen. "Hello, earth to Lavender...anyone in there?" Holly, one of my fellow teachers and best friend, says to me.

We're sitting in my classroom since all of our kids are in the lunchroom and luckily this isn't our week for cafeteria duty. That's probably the only part of my job that I dislike and it's not even because of all the kids. Some of the other teachers are less than pleasant most days. I swear, this place is like high school all over again at times.

"Yes, sorry." I say before taking a bite of the salad that I brought but don't really want. I would kill for some *Wendy's* chicken nuggets right now.

Holly is currently giving me a dirty look. The same one that she's been giving me ever since Rocco started trying to talk to me months ago. It's only gotten worse since Vegas, the pregnancy and well, him announcing to the world that we're together. Let's just say that she's team Rocco all the way.

"So, remind me again why you're still mad at the sweet hot cop who lives with you?" She asks before taking a huge bite of her ham and cheese sub. I'd kill for one of those too, but apparently I'm no longer allowed deli meat.

I look around to make sure that we're entirely alone. "Because he basically called me a whore-ish drunk who sleeps with every man that she comes into contact with."

Okay, I may have – definitely did – over reacted the other night. Again, between the hormones and my brain going on hiatus when I'm in Rocco's presence all alone, I've found that getting mad helps me get away from those piercing hazel eyes. I've already stated that I'm a coward.

She swallows her food and snorts at me. "You know damn well that is not at all what he meant. You were just looking for any reason to hightail it out of there so that you wouldn't do what you actually want to do and jump him."

Have I mentioned that Holly and I have been friends since junior year of high school and roomed together all four years of college?

With us having the same major, we were literally never apart. It's times like this, that it comes back to bite me in the butt.

I sigh and look longingly at her sandwich. She gives me the stink eye and moves it completely out of my reach. "I know that...now."

Once rational thought came back to me, I fully recognized that. But the damage was done. Plus, me pretending to be mad at him, has been keeping him securely on the couch. I really don't know if I could handle sleeping next to that man every night and not accidentally – totally on purpose – end up acting like an octopus.

I use my fork the dig around my unappealing garden salad. "I just don't know what to do Holl. I am so far out of my depth and league with him, that it's not even funny."

She blinks at me and narrows her eyes. "Okay, the depth part I can see since you've never lived with a boyfriend before. What the hell do you mean out of your league? You're hot, sweet...when not preggers, fun and just plain awesome. You're the total package. Any fool within a hundred miles can see that."

"I'm also defective." I mumble. Unfortunately for me, she has freakishly good hearing.

"I swear, I wish that we had gone somewhere else for lunch the day that you met that shit stain Derrick. You have to know that everything that he ever said was untrue and just said to bring you down? He knew that you were way too good for him. Plus, you're obviously not defective if it's a potent alpha hottie doing the seed planting." She says grinning big.

I choke on the cucumber in my mouth. She hits me on the back – hard – dislodging it from my throat. "What in the world is wrong with you!" I hiss but end up coughing.

She hands me my bottle of water with an unapologetic look on her face. "What?" She blinks innocently. "I was just stating that you're not defective for the right man."

I glare at the woman I love like a sister. "You know darn well that's not what you said."

"Opps."

"Opps, my butt! Must you always be so darn inappropriate. We're at work right now."

She shrugs with a wicked grin. "We're all alone. There's no one else to hear about how your lovely garden has been seeded, Lavender dear." She says in a horrible fake British accent.

"No one but the guy who did the planting." We hear drawled from the doorway.

Holly and I both jump and scream at the sound of Rocco's voice. He's leaning against the doorway, in his tight, so very tight, uniform, giving us a huge grin.

I try to hide my shock, the earth could just swallow me up whole right now, I would really appreciate it. I know that I'm bright red. I can feel how hot my face and entire body is. I'm pretty sure that I could melt butter right now. "What are you doing here?" I sputter because life is just so very wonderful today.

He looks at me and takes an unnecessarily long time looking me over from head to toe. I don't know whether to feel alive or dirty. Who am I kidding, I feel both and it's awesome. Shh, hormones, not right now, stay focused. We are at our place of employment surrounded by small children.

He holds up a bag and it takes a few seconds for the red writing to register. Then the smell kicks in, making my stomach rumble and him chuckle. "I saw that you packed a salad this morning but figured that you might want something with a little more sustenance."

"What would make you think that?" I question because I'm obviously the most stubborn person in the world. Why can't I just grab the bag and say thank you?

"Probably because you're sitting there drooling over it and your stomach is giving a lion a run for its money with its growl." Holly mutters before taking a bite of her sandwich.

Rocco ignores the death stare that I'm giving Holly and walks into the classroom. He walks right next to me and squats down. I don't know what's more appealing to me right now, his cologne or the *Wendy's*. My stomach embarrassingly rumbles again...yup it's the *Wendy's*. Nothing can compete with food to a pregnant woman.

Rocco gives me a smirk, almost as if he can read my mind. "Plus, I figured that these chicken nuggets, fries and ranch dressing would get me out of the dog house."

My eyes widen at what he brought and then narrow at him. "How did you know that's what I like?"

His chuckle is deep and gravelly and does absolutely nothing to my core...at all....I swear I'm not lying to myself. "I'm a cop sweetheart. That means that I'm pretty observant. Also, you've ordered the same thing every time that we've stopped there. I could be stupid and still have figured out what you would want."

He's squatting down, so that we are face to face. I can smell his minty breath wash over my face as he speaks. "Oh." I reply like the winner that I have become these days.

Good Lord, I'm a teacher and "oh" is the best that I can come up with? Judging by Holly's snort, she's thinking along the same lines that I am. I am a complete and utter disaster where this man is concerned.

Couldn't he just have one darn flaw? Seriously, it's not normal to be this perfect. What man is this sweet, handsome, caring, thoughtful, sexy, loving, generous, muscular, with great lips and piercing eyes and abs that I want to.... Whoa! I need to stop those thoughts, right there!

I shake my head and give myself a mental slap. I take the bag and give him the best smile that I can muster through my lust filled haze. "Thank you, Rocco. This was very thoughtful."

He gives me his genuine and happy smile. "You're very welcome Lavender." Gah, the way my name rolls off of his tongue does funny things to me.

"Are you still on duty?" I ask, needing to change the subject.

He nods his head. "Yeah, but I let dispatch know my location. So, it's all good. No one will say anything about a police officer patrolling around the school. Who would complain about that?"

He has a point. Most parents would probably be very grateful for it. "I doubt anyone would." I tell him.

"Well, I'm done and need to head back to my classroom to get ready for the little humans to get back." Holly states while getting up and throwing away her trash.

I look at the clock on the wall in a panic, only to realize that we still have twenty minutes left. As if she can sense that I'm about to protest her leaving, because I most certainly am, she states. "I still have some lesson plans that I need to iron out. So, I'm going to use the last twenty minutes of our break," - I don't miss the look she shoots at Rocco and unfortunately, neither does he – "to go over everything. Enjoy your lunch Lav. Nice to see you again Rocco." She says with a huge grin, traitor.

Rocco gives her an equally large grin, obviously sensing that he has an ally. "You too Holly and thanks."

She gives him a wink and blows me a kiss before she leisurely saunters out the door of my classroom. Lesson plans my butt! I can't believe that she's leaving me alone with my sort of live in boyfriend. Okay, that even sounds pitiful to me I think to myself. I really need to get it together where he's concerned.

I look into his mirth filled eyes and just stare. I swear that he has the prettiest eyes that I've ever seen. They're a little bit of green, blue, brown and even yellow all mixed together. It doesn't sound like a good mixture until you get a good look at them. They are absolutely hypnotic. Which is the only reason that I've been staring at him like a doofus for so long.

"As much as I enjoy getting to stare at you as much as I want. You should probably eat your food before it gets cold and unappealing."

My stomach chooses that second to rumble, yet again, causing me to burn even brighter. "Thanks." I mumble as I go through the contents of the bag.

"Anything for you sweet girl." He chuckles lightly. "Mind if I take a seat?" He asks.

Holly and I were sitting at one of the tables used for the kids, since there's more room. Not to mention that my desk is a mess of paperwork. I eye the small chair and then him dubiously. "Are you sure that you'll fit?"

He pulls out a chair that looks miniature compared to his large frame. He purses his lips in a way that is all too appealing. "I'm sure that I can fit. I'm just not so sure that I'll be able to get up without your help."

I snicker. "Then you're going to be stuck there for a while. The kids have more upper body strength than I do." Which is sadly true. I have the upper body strength of a toddler. I've never met a jar that I liked.

"I don't mind being stuck here. At least I have a really nice view." He says with a wink making my blush ramp up about a million degrees. Grrr, he knows exactly what he's doing to me too, if that wicked smirk is anything to go by.

I give him a scolding look that does nothing but make his smile widen. "Shouldn't you be off protecting and serving?"

"I have no problem protecting and serving you, however you want."

I start giggling uncontrollably. He gives me a sheepish look and scratches behind his ear. "Really Rocco?" I laugh even more.

He holds up his hands. "Okay, okay, that one was really cheesy. I'll admit it."

"That was the worst line that I've ever heard!"

He gives me a pout. "It wasn't *that* bad."

"You might as well have asked me what my sign is." I giggle even more until I have to hold my side because of a cramp.

"Okay Miss High and Mighty." He starts before stealing one of my fries and popping it into his mouth. "What are some better lines then?" He asks while still chewing.

I dip one of my fries into the ranch dressing and secretly enjoy the way he wrinkles his nose in disgust. I take a bite of the fry and chew while trying to ignore the way that Rocco's eyes are tracking the movement. "Honestly, anything would've been better than that." I say once I've swallowed the fry. "How in the world have you ever gotten a woman to go out with you before?"

He gives me a dirty look that has absolutely no heat behind it. "I already told you that I've only dated two women within the last few years. And I normally don't really have to try very hard." He gives me another sheepish look that is adorable on him.

"So, you win them over with your stellar personality?" I bat my lashes at him. Where this confidence is coming from, I haven't the slightest idea, but I'll take it. I've never really been the sassy one, Sage has always had that, but Rocco makes me feel like I can say whatever I want without any judgment from him.

He blinks at me a few times and then scoffs. "Please woman, take a look at all of this" – he does a poor Vanna White impersonation across his body – "and tell me that I don't make this uniform look good." He says way too cockily.

I tap my index finger against my lips and pretend to peruse his magnificent body. Does he wear that uniform well? Duh. Am I about to tell him that? Nope. "Hmm, did you end up in the children's section of the uniform store?"

He narrows his eyes at my question. A little birdy with a big mouth – Declan – might've told me how the guys all make fun of him for making sure that his work shirts are always tight. Come to think of it, all of his shirts are tight, not that I mind but still.

"Declan's a bad influence on you." He says calmly with a straight face. "You were so sweet until you became friends with him." He sniffs at me.

I roll my eyes. "Stop being such a baby. The kids I teach act better than all of you guys." I raise an eyebrow but he doesn't even try to defend himself since he knows that I'm right. "If anyone's a bad influence, it's all of you on each other. The six of you are nothing but overgrown children when you're all together."

He crosses his arms over his massive chest, making me wonder if his shirt will be able to hold up. To my disappointment, it does. "We're not that bad." He huffs out.

I smirk and shake my head. "They literally helped you move in, all while ignoring all of my many protests. You all then proceeded to sit outside, making fun of each other the rest of the night. You boys need adult supervision at all times."

"We're all adults." He purses his lips again, making me wish that I could remember what they felt like. "Okay, maybe not Declan, all the time." I raise my eyebrow at him again. "Okay, maybe I'm just as bad some days." He acquiesces. "It's really all Declan though. I was a lot more normal before I met him."

"Okay, fine, I'll give you that one, just because I know how convincing Declan can be when he sets his mind to something."

Rocco nods his head in agreement. That suddenly brings me back to Vegas and Declan shoving Rocco and I in an elevator. "You don't think Declan had anything to do with..." I trail off but point between him and I.

Rocco gives me a grin that causes chills to run down my spine in a not entirely unpleasant way. "Sweetheart, he may have played a role, but I can guarantee you, that nothing happened just because of him. Trust me, I would have no problem reliving Vegas over and over again...except sober this time. I wouldn't want to miss a minute of seeing and feeling you."

And cue me choking on a chicken nugget. What is it with people saying things to me while I'm eating? I take a large gulp of water to push the food down my throat.

"Are you okay?" I would believe the sincerity of his question, if his eyes weren't filled with laughter.

"I'm fine." I mumble. I am so far out of my league when it comes to Rocco, that it's not even funny. I can't even handle innuendos that a normal woman would have a quick comeback for.

"Have dinner with me?" I hear his deep masculine voice ask.

It takes my brain a few seconds to process what the question was. "What?" Is my utterly brilliant reply. You would think that I haven't finished grammar school, let alone am the one teaching it.

He gives me a small, almost nervous smile. "Please come out to dinner with me. As in a real date. We've done all of this kind of backwards."

I can't argue with that. We've really messed this up a bit. I chew on my bottom lip and curiously watch as his eyes track the movement and then darken. Huh.

He leans into me so that I can look into his eyes easily. "Please Lav, give me a chance to show you that I know how to do this the right way. It may have been all rushed but it doesn't mean that it isn't what I really want. Have dinner with me to see if you want to actually give this a shot. If not, I promise I'll leave you alone afterwards, if that's what you want. Just give me one *real* chance." The pleading in his eyes makes my decision for me.

"Okay."

His eyes light up like a kid's on Christmas morning. "I promise that you won't regret this." He places a kiss on my cheek. "Friday at six, be ready sweetheart."

It takes my lust filled hormones a moment to process what he just said. "Wait. Friday? But today is Monday?" I ask confused. He just nods his head with a smile. "Does that mean that I won't see you until Friday too?" I ignore the sharp pang of disappointment that I feel at the thought.

He gives me a cocky grin again. "Sweetheart, we live together, of course you'll see me."

My eyes narrow into slits on their own. "I feel like this is some sort of ploy or something. I feel like I'm being had somehow." I cross my arms.

"I would never play games with you." He leans in, so that his lips are brushing against my ear. "But remember the saying, *All's fair in Love and War* baby."

He smoothly gets up from the tiny chair and bends down to kiss the top of my head. "Have a great rest of your day. See you at home." He throws over his shoulder.

I'm about to give him some sort of reply, once I finish admiring those tight uniform pants. But I'm stopped by a loud squeal. "Uncle Rocco!"

Rocco barely has a second to bend down before Ella is throwing herself into his arms. I look up at the clock on the wall. Shoot! I had lost track of time. Darn man, who looks way too good holding a little girl and twirling her around, with a huge smile lighting his face. I wonder if this is how he'll look holding our baby?

"Hey, Ella Bella." He says before blowing a raspberry into her tummy.

And yes, her mother actually did name her Ella Bella. I swear Kellie has a few screws loose some days. It's a cute name now, but I learned that kids, especially in high school can be cruel.

Her giggles are infectious and cause a smile to break out on my face as I hurry and clean up my lunch. "Uncle Rocco!" She squeals louder. "Stop!" She catches her breath when he relents. "Did you come to see me?" She asks as she smooshes his face together in her little hands.

I take out my phone quickly and pull up my camera app. I'm able to snap a few pictures without anyone seeing. I smile to myself. These will look cute all blown up.

"Of course I came to see my favorite girl." He tells her while giving me a look over her shoulder, that I can't really decipher and truthfully, I'm not sure that I really want to.

"Can you stay with me for the rest of the day?" She asks him.

He shakes his head and pouts comically. "Nope, I have to go back to work and catch some bad guys." He sighs dramatically.

"I wish all the bad guys would just go away already. Then you could spend all day here."

"You and me both kiddo." He says again while staring directly at me.

If I had any self-preservation, I would turn away but I've obviously become a masochist because I just keep watching the man of my dreams get even better. I wonder if it would be weird to start fanning myself?

"Here are all your kids back." Grace Hubert, another teacher, says in her snottiest voice. I swear, I truly don't dislike many people but she is most definitely one of them.

I'm about to reply when I see that she realizes that we have more of an audience than just the kids. I swear, she stands up taller and pushes her boobs out. "Well, hello officer." She purrs with a wicked gleam in her bright gray eyes.

Rocco gives her his professional smile – yes I can tell the difference just don't ask why – and nods his head. "Ma'am."

She waves a hand in the air. "Oh you don't have to call me ma'am. I'm way too young for that." She giggles...actually giggles. I haven't really had any morning sickness but I can feel vomit creeping up my throat.

"I'll just stick to ma'am." He replies politely, but coolly.

I'm totally making him dinner tonight just for the look of shock on her face. If it wasn't so unprofessional and if I was anyone else but me, I would totally go up and kiss that man. I have never seen a man turn her down, including my ex Derrick. He just won himself some major points...darn.

"Oh, umm, well is there something that I can help you with?" She flounders for any excuse to still be standing here.

"He's here to see me." A sassy little voice answers. "He doesn't need help. If he did, he would just ask Miss Lavender." Ella actually rolls her eyes.

If she isn't a little mini-Kellie, I don't know who is. I should also probably reprimand her for being rude but I just can't bring myself to do it. Part of me wants to squeeze and kiss the little sassy girl. I obviously won't, but it doesn't mean that I'm not mentally doing it.

Grace barely holds back her normal sneer when looking at Ella. If she doesn't like me, she likes Kellie even less for some unknown reason. Which is weird because most people who know Kel, absolutely adore her. But she definitely doesn't like Ella just for being her daughter.

Grace looks at me with false concern. "Shouldn't you say something to *your* student?" She looks at me expectantly.

I normally back down because I'm not one for confrontation but seeing her drool over Rocco has, well set my hormones ablaze. I give her a big fake smile and turn to Ella with a real one.

"Ella sweetie, give uncle Rocco a big kiss and hug. It's time for us to start class."

"That's it?" Grace asks in shock.

I can see Rocco grinning into Ella's hair. Ella even has a bit of a smirk on her face. She is actually way too quick and observant for someone her age.

I don't really know what comes over me next. I swear these hormones make you go crazy. Seriously, pregnant women should not be held accountable for their actions. Especially when some cheap and easy woman is sniffing around like a dog in heat.

"Of course not." I smile patiently until she gives a victorious smirk. "Rocco honey, can you pick up some milk on your way home tonight? I finished the last of it with my cereal this morning."

To his credit, he recovers from his obvious shock much quicker than I ever would've. "Sure thing sweetheart. Do you need me to pick anything else up?"

I pretend to think for a moment as Grace's head keeps turning from Rocco to me. I finally shrug when Rocco gives me a look. "Just what you want for dinner. I'll cook tonight." I blow him a kiss and turn to walk back to my desk with my head held high.

Oh boy, what did I just do?

I feel a smack to the back of my head. My hand starts to rub it, as I look around and see Marc standing behind me.

"What the hell did you do that for?" Jesus, he really didn't hold back.

"I can't fucking take it anymore. You've been even more chipper than normal. Ever since Monday afternoon you've been whistling and smiling non-stop. I can't fucking take it anymore. Not only is it annoying, but it's starting to get creepy how happy you are."

"You're such a good friend." I deadpan. "Most friends would be happy that their friend was happy."

"Let's be real here. None of us are normal friends. You want to stalk your woman until she has no other options but you, we're here for you."

We all chuckle when Damon gives Marc the finger and mutters "Everything worked out just fine."

"Yeah bro, that was nothing but smooth sailing." Declan grins.

"She's all mine, isn't she?" Damon stands with his thick arms crossed against his chest.

"You really wonder why she compared you to a serial killer in the beginning?" Marc frowns.

Declan tsks him. "Nu-uh, get it right. Shell said that a serial killer was better."

Marc snaps his fingers at Declan. "Right. Right. My bad. Seriously though, you see no issues?"

"You're the one who came up with the plan to scare her ex." Damon growls. He has a point.

Marc stares at him for a moment. "I'm not the one who gave him a *friendly shove* in the right direction."

"What do you mean *friendly shove*? I thought you said that he ran out in front of that car all on his own?" JJ asks while rubbing his temples.

That's a good question. I always thought that he got scared and just ran in the wrong direction. Damon, Declan and Marc wipe all emotions off of their faces like the creepy bastards that they are and just blink innocently at JJ.

"What do you mean?" Marc asks calmly. "He did run out all by himself."

JJ narrows his eyes and scowls at Marc. "Did he run out or was he pushed out onto the road?"

Marc scratches the back of his head. "Ya know, everything just happened so fast. I just really can't be completely sure about anything that I saw. Plus, it was such a long time ago. Thanks to the kids, my memory is just not what it used to be, ya know?"

JJ looks up at the ceiling and then pinches the bridge of his nose. I watch him turn an interesting shade of red. "Please tell me that you three assholes, didn't push that man out in front of a car?" He asks through severely gritted teeth.

"We didn't push him in front of a car." All three say in unison, robotically. Nah, they haven't practiced that at all.

"Plus, that car came out of nowhere." Declan supplies cheerfully.

"It really was an act of God." Marc tries for solemn.

We all turn and look at Damon, who just stares back at us blankly. "Everyone and their mother knows that I wasn't the least bit broken up about how that day ended."

"I honestly don't know what to do with you guys anymore." He mutters more to himself while shaking his head. He looks at all of us with fire in his eyes. "Just get your shit together and be at the range in twenty minutes!" He yells before storming out of the door.

"You just had to add that, didn't you Mr. Personality?" Marc scolds Damon like he's a child.

"You were the one who insinuated that it wasn't an accident." Damon growls.

Declan just keeps grinning and pretends to shed a tear. "Awe, look at you using such big words. Mom will be so proud."

"You three are exhausting." Morris drawls.

"No, that's your shithead of a wife." Marc replies casually. "She's taken all the fun out of you and left us with a used up robot."

We all look at him like he's lost his mind. "What the fuck are you talking about?" I ask.

Marc waves a hand in the air. "Nothing, sorry. The kids had me watching weird ass alien and robot movies last night since Kay was out with Mason, trying to get him to pick better women or something."

"How'd it go?" Declan asks curiously.

Marc gives us a smirk. "She came home and chugged half a bottle of wine that went straight to her head. I'm guessing she had a bad night with him, but I made up for it."

"None of us needed to know that part." I tell him.

He shrugs unapologetically. "It should because I'm in a great mood, thanks to drunk Kay. But your downright disgusting cheerfulness is making me want to puke. So, what gives? Last I heard, you're still on the couch."

"Can't a guy just be in a good mood?"

"No." Is their unanimous reply.

"Fine." I sigh, knowing that I need to just tell their nosey asses. Plus, we need to get to the range before JJ has a fucking aneurism. "So, Monday I went and brought her lunch."

Declan motions for me to hurry up with his hands. "Yeah, yeah, yeah. We all know this already."

Seriously, I must've been Stalin in a past life to end up with these assholes as friends. "If you'd let me finish, I can explain." I raise an eyebrow as I finish getting dressed. The others seem to realize that they need to as well.

"Anyway, lunch was fine and I convinced her to go out on a real date with me tonight. Then Ella comes in with this other teacher who starts giving Lav an attitude before she spots me."

"I don't see you being happy about that." Damon states while tying his laces.

"I wasn't. But apparently Lavender dislikes her and really disliked it when she started hitting on me. Basically, in one foul swoop she let this chick know that I was taken." I chuckle remembering the look of pure shock on that bitch's face.

Declan, who is finished getting dressed, is leaning up against the lockers with a smirk. "How did Lav do that? She's not overly confrontational. Honestly, chihuahuas have a bigger bite than she does." He's not wrong.

I give him a big smile. "In only the way someone who is sweet can be bitchy." They all give me expectant looks. "She asked me to pick up some milk on my way home and told me to get what I wanted for dinner since she was cooking."

Declan chuckles. "Sage would've been so proud."

I nod my head. "Probably, she even blew me a kiss and walked back to her desk like nothing happened. The look on that chick's face was priceless. So, yeah, I've been happy about her jealously and her telling people that we're together. Though, that was dampened a bit when I spoke to Kellie." I say with a frown while buckling my belt.

"Why?" Morris asks as he finishes and shuts his locker.

"Because her ex cheated on her with this bitch. She also hates Kellie and is pretty mean to Ella. I'm guessing that her hitting on me pushed Lav over the edge so to speak. Well, that and she was trying to be a bitch to Ella. To be honest, that's when I first noticed her back go straight and her eyes narrow."

"That makes sense, since Lavender is friends with your sisters. Just because she generally tries to stay away from conflict, doesn't mean that she'll let someone belittle a child. That's a big no-no when it comes to Lav."

Just thinking back to how my woman stood her ground and wouldn't yell at Ella and then calmly put that bitch in her place, puts a smile on my face. It took all my restraint not to grab her and kiss the hell out of her.

"And tonight I get to start convincing her that we're a good match. She has some fucked up ideas about not being good enough that need to change." I shut my locker and wait for Damon and Marc to finish so that we can leave.

Morris is giving me a frown. "Wait, she doesn't think that you're good enough for her? After everything that you've done for her?" He asks incredulously.

I shake my head. "No, she's convinced that she's boring and not as pretty as someone that she thinks that I should be with. Well, that's what I've gotten from conversations with her and some with Sage."

"Has she not looked in a mirror?" Marc asks. "Dogs don't exactly howl when she walks past." He jokes trying to get me to smile.

"Her ex fucked with her head and self-esteem." Declan says seriously while glaring at the wall. "She legitimately thinks that she's boring, ugly, defective and whatever other shit he told her for years. Trust me, years of putting someone down can do damage to even the most confident people."

I nod my head. "Yeah, that's why I'm trying to make tonight all about her. To show her that she deserves all the good things that he told her that she didn't."

"He called her defective?" Damon asks in a low voice.

Here's where I should be a good person and a good police officer and tell Damon no or even change the subject But I've always said that I try to be a good person, I just don't always succeed.

"Yup." I answer getting creepy smiles from Marc and Declan. Morris is just shaking his head and pretending to wash his hands of this conversation. Damon looks...thoughtful, which is probably the most disturbing of them all. Too late to turn back now though.

"Hmm." Is Damon's response before walking out the door.

"This is either going to be a lot of fun or really bad." Marc says with too much enthusiasm.

"Let's go." I say. "No need to piss JJ off any more than we're about to." I sigh.

Declan walks up and throws an arm around my neck. "Just think of it as team building exercises. He'll have to like the fact that we all work so well together."

"I'm sure he'll be thrilled when this guy ends up in a hospital bed too." Morris drawls.

Marc rolls his eyes before shutting his locker and walking over to us. "You worry too much. I swear you were fun before you married my sister. And last time was just a simple miscalculation. We'll obviously plan better this time around."

"That makes me feel a lot better." I tell him.

He looks at me in surprise. "Really?"

"No, if anything I'm one hundred percent certain that we're either going to land in one of our own cells or lose our jobs."

"Or the major concern of someone dying, but hey that's just me I guess." Morris shrugs.

"No one died last time." Declan replies blandly.

Morris hold up his index finger and thumb. "The motherfucker came this close to death." He holds his fingers in front of Declan's face who just swats them away. "Seriously, how is no one else worried?" He looks around at us before storming out.

"What's up with him?" I ask while tilting my head to the door. "He's usually pretty easy going. He's been on edge for days."

Marc chuckles and rolls his eyes. "Mellie has decided that she wants to lose all the baby weight that she gained when she decided to eat for ten instead of two. But my sister couldn't just be miserable by herself, nope, not that shithead. She decided to put her poor sucker of a husband on a diet too."

"He's actually doing it?" Declan laughs.

"Not at first." Marc replies. "He would sneak whatever when away from her. But she's like a damn bloodhound when it comes to junk food now. She sniffed it out and had a meltdown. The poor bastard has been doing it ever since."

"Why doesn't she just work out more so that she can still eat some of what she wants?" I ask. It makes the most sense, instead of depriving herself of everything that she wants.

Marc and Declan just stare at me. "What?" Damn, it was just a question.

"Have you met my train wreck of a sister? Granted, the girl can shoot and ride a quad better than most people. But she has absolutely no coordination when it comes to actual exercise. I have literally watched her fall off a fucking treadmill that wasn't even going that fast. If she tries to exercise, she might end up killing herself and anyone unfortunate enough to be near her."

I rub the back of my head. I forgot that for some reason Mellie is great at certain things, while just awful at normal everyday life. Watching her walk around while pregnant was terrifying just because she wobbled so much. Oddly enough though, she was actually really graceful during her pregnancies.

"Right, never mind. So, he's just going to be miserable for a while?"

"Yup." Marc chirps with a gleam in his eyes that doesn't bode well for Morris.

"Come on, let's get this day over with. I have a woman to win over tonight."

Marc walks to the door and holds it open for us. "Ya know, generally speaking, most men don't have to win over the woman that they've already knocked up."

Declan and I walk out and turn to look at the tall jackass. "Your point?" I huff.

He gives me a cheesy grin. "Nothing buddy." He says with a hard slap to my back. "Just wishing you some luck. You're probably going to need it."

He's such an asshole.

Several Hours Later:

I feel like a kid on my first date. Granted, tonight is probably one of the most important nights of my life. So far, everything has gone smoothly. I went home after work and ended up getting there at the same time as Lavender. We both stood awkwardly in the living room making small talk for ten minutes before I told her that I was going to take a quick shower.

It was weird, we've never been that awkward before while here together. I think that both of us were definitely feeling the first date jitters. Luckily by the time that we were both finished getting ready, the awkwardness had seemed to dissipate a bit.

We had a quiet dinner at the Italian place in town and now we're walking around downtown, through the large park. It's a warm spring night, so I thought that she might enjoy taking a stroll, especially after all of the food we ate.

Lav ate all of her fettucine alfredo and some of my chicken parm. The best part was that she had zero guilt about it and even ordered dessert. There is nothing more annoying than taking a woman out to eat and having her order a fucking salad. I don't know who told them that men like it when they eat like a bird in front of us, but we don't.

Now we're walking down by the waterfront, enjoying the warm salty air. The smell of the ocean, mixed in with Lavender's candy scent, is driving me crazy. To make it even worse for my poor unused dick, she's in a curve hugging dress that keeps blowing up with the wind...just not as much as I would like. Her hair is down and looks wild because of the wind. Her cheeks are flushed and her eyes are bright. She is literally the most beautiful woman that I've ever seen.

"You're staring." She says shyly with a small smile.

I didn't even realize that we had stopped walking and that I was staring at her. "I'm sorry. I was just thinking about how you are the most beautiful woman that I've ever seen and how lucky I am that you're here with me."

Even with the low lighting, I can see her entire face turn bright red. She tucks a piece of hair behind her ear. "Thank you." She mutters looking down at her feet.

I see a bench up ahead and walk towards it while holding onto her hand. We both take a seat when we reach it. I wrap my left arm around her shoulders and she automatically snuggles into me like we've done it a thousand times before. I never knew the meaning of perfection, until this very moment.

"Thank you for tonight Roc." She says while looking up at me. "It's been a really long time since I've had such a great night."

I kiss her temple. "I'm glad sweetheart, you deserve it and more." I tell her honestly.

She sits up a bit. "No, I really don't." She says while biting on her bottom lip. "I have been so awful to you this entire time."

I give her a small smile. "I wouldn't say awful."

She narrows her eyes at me and huffs. "I told Declan to put your belongings back at your place when he asked me where to put them."

I can't help it, between the sad little pout on her face and remembering her little sassy voice saying that to Declan, I start cracking up. I actually have tears streaming down my face and a cramp in my side when I'm able to get control over myself again.

"This is not funny Rocco, I was so mean." She covers her face with her hands.

"Honey," I remove her hands from her face and hold them in my own, "you weren't even close to being mean. We all ignored everything that you had to say. If anything, I would say that you were way too nice to all of us. Hell, most people would've called the cops." I chuckle.

She gives me a droll look. "You are the cops."

I nudge her with my shoulder. "You know what I mean. I can guarantee that no one thought that you were mean. You on a bad day, is Sage on a good one."

She rolls her eyes with a smile. "I swear my sister wouldn't know how to keep her mouth shut to save her life. She had to have been switched at birth. No one else in the family is as confrontational as she is."

I snigger to myself when I think about her parents. Confrontational...definitely not. Complete and utter hippies....yup. I'm pretty sure that her parents tried to get JJ's parents to do a wife swap type of thing. And everyone thinks Dee is bad when it comes to hitting on younger men. Hell, Dee looked tame compared to Sage and Danny's parents at the wedding.

"What's that look on your face about?" She asks with a grin. That's another thing that I've seemed to accomplish lately, Lav is a lot more comfortable around me now.

I give her a smirk. "I was just thinking about yours and Danny's parents at the wedding."

Her eyes widen so much that it's comical. "Oh my gosh, please don't remind me!" She screeches. "They have to be the most embarrassing parents in the entire universe. Sage and I pleaded with them to behave themselves. They even swore to us that they would be on their best behavior. We even confiscated all of their weed so that they would be good and not do anything crazy."

I choke on my saliva and cough into my hand. "You had to steal your parents' weed? You know that they smoke it?"

She rolls her pretty eyes at my question. "They wear hemp and live in a nudist colony. It doesn't take a rocket scientist to figure out that they probably smoke weed." She starts biting on a fingernail and mutters. "We just didn't take into account what they would be like with only alcohol."

I chuckle lowly. "They were entertaining, that's for sure."

"I'm pretty sure that JJ's parents are scarred for life because of them."

I decide to change the subject instead of lie to her because I'm pretty sure that she's right. "So, is there anything else that you want to do tonight?"

When I look at her, she's bright red again and chewing furiously at her bottom lip. "I want to go home."

"Okay." I say and watch her continue to fidget nervously.

"To bed."

"Okay, I'm sure that you're tired after a long day." I try to say in an upbeat manner to hide my disappointment that tonight is ending already.

"I'm not tired Rocco and I don't want you to sleep on the couch anymore." She says quietly.

I'm so mesmerized watching her chew on her lip that it takes me a few seconds to process what she just said. My eyes fly up to hers and see that she's staring at me.

"You don't want me to sleep on the couch anymore?" I ask to make sure that I heard her correctly and that my brain isn't playing tricks on me.

She shakes her head no. "I need to hear you say it Lav. This is one of those times that I want to make sure that you are one hundred percent on board with this."

I stare into her eyes as I deliver my next words "Because once we do this, there is no going back. I'm already all yours, but after tonight, you'll be mine, all mine sweetheart. So, take a minute to think about if this is what you really want." When I'm finished I can feel every nerve ending on my body begin to stand

I feel like I'm about to jump out of my skin. I want this more than anything but I want her to be sure. I already know that she's it but I don't want her to ever have any doubts about me.

She gives me a half shy and half confident smile. "I'm absolutely sure that this is what I want, Rocco."

And that's all I needed to hear.

Oh my gosh, what in the world was I thinking? Well, I know what I was thinking. My hormones were in control and thought that it would be a great idea to get Rocco all to ourselves...naked. Now though, my brain is back in control – mainly – and I am freaking out.

It has been a long time since someone, other than myself and my doctor, has seen me naked. I don't count Vegas for obvious reasons. Some of that tequila would be great right about now. And I've gained weight since becoming pregnant. My stomach is definitely not flat-ish anymore. It is definitely puffy now.

We were both quiet for most of the drive home, which did not help out my nervousness at all. Nope, all that did was give me time to think about what all those women who hit on him look like.

That just caused me to freak out even more knowing that I'm what most people call a bit thick. I'm not fat per se, but my legs are not twig like at all. I have big boobs and a butt that resembles a big bubble.

I'm normally comfortable with my body, but those other women are pretty much as close to perfect as you can get. Tall, thin, perky boobs, rock hard abs and a firm butt. There is no way that I'm going to be able to even come close to looking as good as one of those women.

We're currently standing in the living room staring at each other awkwardly for the second time tonight. Geesh. You would think that as adults, things wouldn't be so awkward. I mean, I know why I'm feeling awkward but I don't know why he's gone so quiet.

Crud! What if he's having second thoughts and is trying to figure out a way to tell me? I don't know which I want more, for him to tell me that he's changed his mind or for us to actually go through with this.

I know which one my hormones want, but those traitorous things cannot be trusted. They're the whole reason that we're standing here like this right now after a wonderful evening.

"Those are some crazy thoughts judging by the looks crossing your face sweetheart." Rocco chuckles in a deep gravelly tone that makes my core clench. "If you're having second thoughts, it's okay. We can take this all slower."

"Yes. No. That's not." I huff and blow out a breath of air. "I'm not having second thoughts, but I'm afraid that you are." I say, somehow managing to hold his stare the entire time. I need to see his reaction to make sure that he's not just being nice.

His head jerks back like I just slapped him and his eyes widen. "You think that I was having second thoughts?" He sounds like he's choking. "Honey, it's taking everything in me not to just pick you up and throw you over my shoulder. I can guarantee you that I'm thinking a lot of things regarding you and none of them are about this not happening. You still wearing clothes is actually killing me right now."

If his words alone can make my body come alive, I'm almost frightened to know what the rest of him can do to me. Rocco is extremely potent when it comes to my hormones. I subconsciously lick my lips and watch his eyes darken as he tracks the movement.

Rocco is staring at me like he wants to devour me whole. I suddenly feel like Little Red Riding Hood, standing in front of the Big Bad Wolf, only I want to be devoured mind, body and soul. His predatory gaze is as terrifying as it is exciting.

He takes a step towards me and grins when I hold my ground. Tonight is a night for new beginnings for us. This will signify that we are both all in on this crazy ride together, but it also means that I'm going to leave the old Lavender behind.

I'm not going to let Derrick and his awful words ruin another moment of my life, especially when everything that I've ever wanted for my future is standing in front of me, looking at me like I'm the only thing in this entire world that he sees.

He walks forward and stops in front of me. He lowers his face so that our lips are almost touching. "Whatchya thinking about sweetheart?" His breath mingles with my own.

I take a deep breath and give him what Sage would call a wicked smirk. "I'm wondering what it's like to be eaten by the Big Bad Wolf." I whisper against his lips.

I can tell the moment that he catches onto what I meant because his eyes turn black. With what can only be described as an animalistic growl, he picks me up and throws me carefully over his shoulder. "You'll find out in a few minutes."

He gracefully strides towards my, well now our bedroom and gently places me on the bed. My fluffy down comforter feels like a gigantic cloud and I feel as though I'm staring at heaven. Rocco is looming over me like an other worldly god. I think that he's probably built better than any statue that I've ever seen.

He starts to unbutton his light green dress shirt, slowly, while staring at me the entire time. I can feel myself getting wetter with each button that he undoes. Much to my dismay, once he opens up his shirt, I see that he has a white undershirt on as well.

He takes off the dress shirt completely and ever so slowly removes his undershirt. His chest and abs look like they were carved out of granite. He gives me what could only be considered a salacious grin.

"What's wrong Little Red, cat got your tongue?" The deep gravel of his voice causes me to rub my legs together.

"I'm pretty sure that I swallowed my tongue when you took your shirt off." I mumble absentmindedly much to his delight, if his wide grin is anything to go by.

He unbuttons his pants but goes no further and I can't even stop the pout that comes to my face. He leans down and runs his hands down my calves and removes my flats for me. His touch is warm and electric, I actually feel the tiny hairs on my body standing.

He rubs up and down my legs and stops when he reaches the edge of my dress. He holds onto the bottom of it and raises his eyebrows at me. This is it, this is the moment that everything truly changes and I couldn't be anymore ready for it.

I nod my head and lift my arms, allowing him to remove the dress in one tug. I send up a mental high five to Sage for picking out this lingerie set for me. It's all black lace with cute little pink bows in between my breasts and on each side of my hips.

"If this is another dream, I never want to fucking wake up." He says in a breathless moan.

I narrow my eyes at the gorgeous specimen of alpha male in front of me. "We've talked about you curbing your language."

He gives me a big smile. "Good to know that this isn't a dream."

"How do you know that?" I question.

He leans in close so that his lips are only centimeters from my own. "Because in my fantasies, your mouth is worse than mine."

He doesn't give me even a second to process that before his lips are on mine. This isn't a regular kiss, this is a branding, he's telling me that I'm his and only his. His tongue caresses my own with a firm pressure that makes my entire body melt into the comforter.

He lays himself on top of me, but keeping most of his weight off using his arms. I slide my hands through his hair, while also wrapping my legs around his waist. I don't want to know where he ends and I start.

While still kissing me, he runs one hand up my side and behind my back. I feel the snap of my bra detaching from the clasp. I can't help but let my hands roam around his sculpted back, feeling his muscles ripple with every move that he makes.

I moan loudly when he breaks the kiss. "Don't worry sweetheart. It's just time for you to find out what it's like to be eaten alive."

My body burns even brighter with his words but not just from embarrassment. Nope, my hormones are in control and they want him to devour me whole. My entire body is so wired that I'm actually shaking with anticipation.

Rocco, of course, doesn't disappoint. He starts kissing down my neck while simultaneously removing my bra. I gasp when he encloses one nipple with his mouth. He looks up at me in questions while still licking and twirling his tongue around one nipple and then the other.

Between each rapid breath and gasp I manage to explain. "Pregnancy hormones." I moan loudly as he bites down just enough to cause a hint of pain. "My whole body is super sensitive right now due to hormones."

"Hmmm." He murmurs as he continues his wonderful assault on my body.

Why in the world have I not let him do as he pleased with me all these months? Hormones are amazing, I'm sorry I ever said anything bad about you guys.

Rocco continues to make his way down my body to where I'm dying for him the most. He gets to my panties and literally takes them off with his teeth. Can a person spontaneously cum while watching something, because I'm pretty sure that I just did?

My breaths are coming out in rapid pants. I feel like I've just run a marathon and he's barely gotten started. I might not survive him, but it will be a great way to go.

He runs his hands all over my legs until he reaches my knees and then pushes them apart, allowing himself enough room to fit. And cue me blushing furiously. I try to close my legs, which is stupid considering he's in between them currently.

I jump at the first feel of his breath on my core. He looks up at me and grins while placing an arm over my hips, effectively holding me in place to be at his mercy. He holds himself right above my core, not moving, just breathing. Every breath makes me clench and vibrate with need.

"Rocco, please." I whine not even recognizing my own voice.

"Just making sure that this is what you want." He chuckles darkly.

"You know it is. Please, move, do anything, you're killing me right now." I say while trying to close my legs to no avail just to get some sort of friction.

"We can't have you dying on me." He says right before I feel his tongue lick from bottom to top. He circles my clit with his tongue and if it wasn't for his arm holding me down, I'm pretty sure that I would've reached the ceiling.

I now know for a fact that I should've listened to my hormones all of those times that they told me to jump onto Rocco and never let him go. Mentally, I can't even comprehend the amount of pleasure that is currently flowing through my body.

Every lick and suck ramps my body up higher and higher. My thighs are clamped around his head and my hands are grabbing fistfuls of the comforter. I can feel that I'm so close to the edge but I just can't go over.

"I need." I gasp incoherently.

"I've got you honey, don't worry." He says while sliding one and then two fingers into me.

Between his fingers stretching me and the vibration from his words, that's all it took. I can feel my body clamp down on his fingers, causing them to stop moving. My entire body goes tight, right before wave after wave of pure bliss comes over me.

I'm not even sure how long my climax lasts. I'm guessing it's a little while, considering when I finally open my eyes again, Rocco is fully naked. I can't even comprehend the perfection that is Rocco, naked and fully erect.

He watches me, as I watch him, his eyes never leaving me. He takes himself in his hand and starts pumping up and down slowly. If I thought that he was fully hard before, I was mistaken. He gets harder and harder each second. I have never seen anything more erotic than him watching me while I watch him.

I have just had one of the most powerful, if not the most powerful orgasm of my entire life and it feels as if nothing happened. My body is strung tighter than a bow again, causing me to rub my legs together in anticipation of having him inside of me.

"Are you ready for this sweetheart? There's no going back after this." He asks, and I know that he's not just referring to this physical act, but to everything in our lives.

I give him the only answer that comes to mind. "I've never been so ready in my entire life." I reply.

It's true, my body, mind and soul have never been as ready as they are for him. Judging from his megawatt smile, he understands me completely.

He positions himself between my legs once again, legs that I hadn't even thought to close in the first place since he short circuited my brain, and I can feel him at my entrance.

He holds himself up on his arms once again and just stares into my eyes. I smile, nod and place my lips on his as he begins to enter me. He slides in slowly, but even still I suck in a deep breath. It's been a really long time and he is definitely a lot bigger than Derrick was.

It takes a few moments once he's fully in for me to get used to his size. Once the burning dulls down from being stretched and the pleasure starts, I move my hips to let him know that he's okay to start moving.

He gets the clue and starts a slow pace of moving in and out. I wrap my legs around him and place my arms around his back. Every thrust starts pushing me closer and closer to the edge again.

I try to keep up as he increases his pace, but once it turns furious, I pretty much just hang on for the ride.

I'm sure that I'll be mortified later on when I remember moaning "faster" and "harder" every few moments to him. But right now the only thing that I care about is chasing the feeling that's almost within my reach, a reach that I keep missing.

I whine and sound like a dog to my own ears but I still don't care. "I've got you Lav." He states as he circles a finger around my clit.

I've never understood the term, going off like a rocket, until this very moment. Because that's exactly what I do now. I feel like I've just rocketed to space and shattered into a million different pieces.

As I'm coming back down to earth, I'm vaguely aware of Rocco muttering a curse and stilling above me. In one move, he's rolled us to where I'm now laying on his chest with his arms wrapped around me. Let's not forget that he's still inside of me and somehow still hard. Geez, my stupid hormones have been right all along.

We're both breathing like we've just run the New York City Marathon. His breathing causing me to bounce up and down on his chest, making me giggle.

"What's so funny pretty girl?" He asks with a smile in his voice.

"The way you're breathing, is making me feel like I'm on a bouncy castle. Only a very muscular one."

He chuckles but slows his breathing down. He's rubbing my back with both hands. I'm already so relaxed that I can feel myself drifting off to sleep. That's probably the only reason why I answer his next question happily, without freaking out in the slightest, well at least until I wake up the next morning.

"Hey honey?" He says in a low, soothing voice. "Do you think that we can go to my parents' house for dinner tomorrow to tell them the good news?"

"Sure." I yawn before snuggling into his chest deeper. "That sounds like a lot of fun."

That's the last thing I remember until I wake up the next morning and have a complete freak out – hidden in my bathroom – about meeting his parents and telling them I'm pregnant. I'm sure that I won't seem like the world's biggest tramp, what-so-ever.

That Evening:

I wonder if I'm too young to have a heart attack? Because I'm pretty sure that I'm in the process of having one. I have been searching my closet for the past two hours for something appropriate to wear to dinner that doesn't scream trashy.

Who am I kidding? I'm that stupid cliché. I literally got pregnant during one night in Vegas. I can't believe that my life has turned into some joke. And worse yet, we have to tell his parents, his very Catholic parents, that we are having a baby without being married.

I know that it's 2019 and that it's not that big of a deal. But it kind of is when you have to tell the parents of the man that you may or may not – even my subconscious snorts - want to marry someday, that you turn easy thanks to tequila.

And why can't I find one darn thing to wear? I've literally taken out every item that I own and nothing looks good enough. Maybe I should just tell him that I'm not feeling well and have him go by himself.

I already stated that I'm a coward. I am not above letting him tell them all by himself. I remember how much Kellie said that they freaked out when she told them that she was pregnant.

I won't be able to handle it if they look at me with disdain or say some of the things that other people have said over the years about Sage. It just stinks that no one ever says anything bad about the guy. It's always the woman's fault, like the guy had no clue what he was doing.

Okay, okay, no need for those thoughts. I can be positive about this. Sure his parents will probably be upset and maybe even think that I did this on purpose to trap him. Crud...no bad thoughts. Only happy, positive ones.

Positive thoughts. Ahh, yes, my parents were really happy when I called to tell them. Granted, not much makes them upset, especially not more babies. My parents may not be your typical everyday parents, but I can say this about them, they are amazingly supportive.

Honestly, they are probably some of the world's best parents to have. They are always happy and welcoming. They supported Sage and Danny without a moment's hesitation and never once did they utter words of disappointment. They may be hippies, and I won't exactly just leave my child with them, especially on the weekends, but they are two of the most loving parents that anyone could ever ask for.

I take a deep breath and grab a nice pair of jeans and a light pink sweater. I can do this. It doesn't matter what anyone else thinks. My family is happy and supportive of me, I have an incredible man who bulldozed his way into my life and I'm going to have a precious baby that I never thought I would. All in all, I'm doing very well in life right now.

After another few calming breaths, I get dressed and have a seat on the bed to put my ballet flats on. I look up when I hear a creak and see Rocco leaning against the door jam. His muscular arms are crossed over his chest and he has a small smile gracing his handsome face.

"I thought that I was going to have to dress you myself." He states with a mischievous smile. "Not that I would've minded but I'm glad that you did it on your own."

I look up and give him a nervous smile. "I'm just worried that your family is going to be upset with me."

I twist my fingers together while biting my bottom lip. I really need to try to break this nasty habit.

His eyes widen. "Why would my family be upset with you sweetheart? If anything, they'll be mad at me for keeping you all to myself for so long."

I give him a weary smile. "You didn't really have much choice in the matter."

He shrugs his large shoulders carelessly. "I could've been pushier. I figured it was best to give you some space."

I can feel my eyes get large and my mouth gapes open. "Telling everyone that we're together and moving yourself in was what you consider giving me space?" I ask incredulously.

He chuckles gravelly and I pretend that it does absolutely nothing to my core. Now is definitely not the time to be thinking sexy thoughts about him, when I'm about to meet his parents.

"Oh honey, you have no idea what I'm capable of when I set my mind to something. You're lucky that I'm not as devious as the rest of our friends are. They told me that I should just a find a way to marry you without you knowing."

"Who in the world would suggest something like that? It's completely insane!" I screech.

"Your sister and Kay."

My lips thin. I don't even have a reply because now thinking about it, that sounds exactly like something that they would suggest.

"And Holly."

"Looks like I'm in need of a new best friend." I mutter darkly causing him to laugh.

The man has an amazing laugh. I just sit here and soak up the glorious sound. His eyes light up like the sun and give an almost boyish, carefree look to him. I actually hear myself sigh. My hormones are out of control.

"You ready to get going honey?" He asks while at the door.

I give him the brightest smile that I can muster, which in truth isn't overly bright. "Yup." I nod and stand. "I'll be out in two minutes. I just need to put the final touches on."

He gives me a wink. "You already look gorgeous, but do what ya gotta do." He shrugs before walking out of the room.

I slump against my dresser once he's out of sight. I send up a silent prayer that things go well tonight. I really don't want his family upset with him over me.

I finish getting ready and take a deep breath before leaving my room. Here goes nothing.

We've been at my parent's house for over an hour now and Lavender is just starting to relax. I know that she worked herself up into a near panic attack, so I'm actually happy that she's starting to finally calm down. With the way that she clutched my hand when we first walked in, you would think that my family were a bunch of serial killers.

I tried telling her not to worry because I was sure that they would all love her. Did she listen to me though? Nope. She worked herself up into a tizzy as Ma would say. She's already friends with two of my sisters. I don't know why she was freaking out so damn much.

And just like I told her, my mother was beyond ecstatic to meet her. Hell, my mom bypassed me completely and run up to Lav and wrapped her in a huge hug. My dad actually had to pry her off of my shell-shocked woman. Luckily, he kept it short and sweet with a kiss on the cheek.

According to my sister Kellie, Lav has a huge, mini-fan in my niece. Apparently, all she talks about when she gets home from school is how wonderful Ms. Lavender is. Not that I disagree, but poor Lav hasn't been left alone at all. Between my mother and niece, I'm starting to worry that they're coming up with a plan to kidnap Lav for themselves.

I'm kidding...mostly...I don't put much past my mother.

We're all sitting around the dining room table after having just finished eating dinner. I swear my mother makes the best corned beef and cabbage in the world. We devoured everything and I'm pretty sure that I'm going to have to be rolled out of here tonight. But damn that was good as hell.

My mother has been giving me a questioning look all night. She's sensed how nervous Lav is and can't figure out why, but she knows something's up. I wanted Lav to be relaxed before we tell them about the baby.

I know that my sweet woman is convinced that my mother will be upset and want nothing to do with her. Poor Lav has no idea that we're about to make my mother's year and that she'll probably attach herself to Lavender like a leech until the baby gets here.

I grab Lav's hand under the table and squeeze it twice. She looks at me with trepidation written all over her beautiful face. I give her a smile and turn to my parents, who are in no way, shape or form, creepily watching us.

I clear my throat a few times suddenly nervous, even though I know that everyone will be happy and excited for us. "We've got something that we want to tell you all."

Luckily, it's just my parents, Ella, and my sisters. I figured that everyone all at once might be too much for Lav. My other two sisters left their husbands and kids at home. I chuckle to myself. I barely had to ask them to leave everyone at home before they were yelling sure. I knew damn well that those two would have no problem with a kid free night.

"I knew it!" Amy yells. "You two got married when you were in Vegas!"

My mom's already clapping like a demented seal without us even saying yes. Lavender is choking a little.

"No, we didn't get married in Vegas." I tell them all.

They all look disappointed, except for Kellie. She's been giving me a sly smile all night. "I think I know what it is." Kellie chirps. "Hmm, not everything that happens in Vegas, stays in Vegas huh?"

"Ah, what do you mean?" Lavender asks while turning a cute shade of red.

Kellie puts down the fork that she was playing with and steeples her fingers on the table. Everyone else is watching with rapt attention.

"You know, Ella was so worried about you." Kellie tells her.

Lavenders eyes get huge. "Why was she worried about me?" My poor woman fell into that one, hook, line and sinker.

Kellie's eyes gleam with delight. "Well, she was so worried about you getting sick all of the time. Having to run out of the room to throw up...for weeks. And then, what do ya know, I find out that my big brother has been sniffing around you for months before hand." Kel taps a finger on her lips really playing this up for everyone. "So, Lav, how's that stomach flu been treating you?"

And cue my mom jumping up and down and clapping like a demented seal once again. My father isn't trying to hold her in place at this moment. He knows damn well that once she gets the confirmation that she's after that she'll be out of that chair in no time.

Lavender's lips are pursed knowing damn well that she walked right into this one. "It's better now, thanks." She's staring my sister down with retribution shining in her eyes.

Kellie being completely unperturbed just gives her a victorious smirk. "Hmm, that's good. How long did it last...about twelve to thirteen weeks would you say?"

I just shake my head at these two. Everyone else is literally on the edge of their seats and these two are keeping up with this dumb charade.

Lavender narrows her eyes at my sister and mutters. "Something like that."

And that was all it takes before complete pandemonium breaks out. My sisters are jumping up and down while hugging me. My mom has Lavender in a death grip, like her and her future grandbaby will disappear if she gives her any breathing room. I probably should've given Lav a heads up about how much of a hugger my mother is, I muse. I internally shrug, oh well, too late now.

My dad is still sitting at the table with a smile and look of contentment on his face. He's been the only one to stay put, thank God. I look over at him and receive a wink.

My dad and I were finally able to escape once all the women started talking about pregnancy and showers and a bunch of other shit that we had absolutely no interest in.

We snuck out to his workroom in the garage. For as long as I can remember, my dad has always had a beater car in here that he would tinker with. Personally, after growing up in a house full of women, I think he just needed to escape.

Dad pulls two beers out of the fridge and hands me one. We both clink our bottles after opening them. "Congratulations son, I'm happy for you." He tells me before taking a seat on his work bench and motioning for me to do the same.

I sit down and take a sip of my beer. "Thank you. We're pretty excited about it."

"So, how'd you get her to finally give you the time of day?" He chuckles at the look of shock on my face.

"What makes you think that I had to do the chasing? What if she was the one chasing me?" I defend. It could've happened like that.

His lips twitch. "Son, you have a tiny little spy in the form of a niece. That girl has been telling all of us all year about how you try to talk to her teacher and fail miserably. Hell boy, why do you think after the first few times that you went there, that you were asked almost every other day to go pick up Ella?"

I raise an eyebrow. "You all were trying to help me?"

He nods and sips his beer. "We tried but damn you kept failing. Honestly, we started to think that it was a lost cause. The only reason we kept sending you, is because your mother had her heart set on that sweet teacher and you becoming an item."

"Remind me to thank Mom for being the only one who had faith in me."

He fucking snorts so hard that he actually chokes on a sip of beer. "She didn't have any faith in you." He coughs. "She was actually considering just going up to that school and talking to that girl herself. Thank Kellie for convincing your mother that she would probably scare the poor girl away instead of reeling her in."

Note to self: babysit Ella for an entire weekend for Kellie.

"So, how did you end up finally getting her to give you the time of day?" He asks with a smirk.

"Tequila." I respond without thinking.

"Son, you better explain yourself. You aren't too old to receive an ass whooping. You better not have gotten that girl drunk on purpose. Boy, I will beat you into next year."

My father would too. Even for a man who's getting older, he's still in great shape. I have no doubt that he would give me a run for my money.

"That's not what I meant but I'm glad to know that you think so highly of me." I deadpan.

His eyes turn into slits. "All you said was tequila. What the fuck was I supposed to think?"

I hold my arms out at my side. "That I would have to get a woman drunk to get her into bed!" I shout.

He holds up his hand in surrender. "Fine then, what actually happened?"

I scratch the back of my neck and cough into my hand. "We both got drunk in Vegas and ended up in bed." I rush out in a mumble.

My dad blinks a few times, while his beer is paused midway to his mouth. "You want to repeat that last part son? Cause I'm pretty sure that you just told me the same thing that you were so offended about."

"No, I was offended that you thought that I would purposely get her drunk." I grit out. "What I'm telling you, is that that we both remember drinking with Declan, him pushing us into an elevator and then waking up naked in bed together."

He takes a long pull of his beer and looks at me thoughtfully. "So, your buddy basically got you both drunk in hopes that you two would screw like rabbits and that she would start to like you? And because you both were piss drunk, you forgot to use a condom and ended up pregnant? Am I missing anything?"

I suck on the inside of my cheek debating on whether or not I should tell him everything and then decide to just say fuck it. "You missed where she ignored me for a few weeks after Vegas."

He purses his lips. "I have a feeling that I really don't want to know, but now I need to." He sighs and rubs his temple. "How did you get her to stop ignoring you after Vegas?"

I tug on my right ear and give him a sheepish look that he rolls his eyes at. "So, with the blessing of her sister, mind you," - I say like I'm not to admit that I went full blown creeper – "I told everyone that we were together and moved myself into her place. Which for the record was her sister Sage's idea."

He just blinks rapidly for a full minute without moving the rest of his body. He looks down at his beer and then back at me. He shakes his head and gets up from the bench. "Yeah, I'm going to need something a bit stronger for the rest of this conversation."

"It's not that bad."

He stops walking and turns to look at me. "Not that bad? Son, is she even here of her own free will or did you kidnap the poor girl? Does she have some form of Stockholm syndrome now? Is that why you felt safe leaving her in the house?"

"Ha, ha...you're so funny."

He raises an eyebrow before continuing his search for his bottle of Johnny Walker Black. "I'm not completely joking." He mutters while taking the bottle out of his hiding spot that everyone in the family knows about.

"Of course she's here because she wants to be." I scoff. "It just took some convincing...that's all."

"So, ya'll are living together?" He asks while pouring himself a hefty glass.

I nod. "Yeah, we've finally started working everything out. I literally just got her to admit that she wants to be with me too. Apparently, her ex was a real piece of shit who treated her badly. She's been skittish to say the least." I ground out.

"Yeah, I've met Derrick a few times. It wasn't a pleasure, I can tell you that." My dad says surprising the shit out of me.

"How do you know about her ex?" I question, causing him to look at me like I'm stupid.

He takes a sip of his whiskey and gives me a look. "I asked around about her," - meaning a few cop buddies at the station – "and heard all about how she's an angel from above and how he treated her like garbage and cheated on her."

"When was this?" I ask while holding the beer between my hands.

"When your mother convinced herself that this girl would be her daughter-in-law, come hell or high water." He chuckles and I join him. He's about to take a sip of his drink when he pauses. "You met her parents?"

I laugh at the look on his face. "Yeah, they're something all right. You would never guess that her and Sage are related to them...that's for sure."

His lips twitch. "No, I suppose no one ever would. They okay with all of this?"

I snort recalling the other day when I spoke to her parents. "Yup. They told me that I should just take her to Vegas and get married. Even offered to supply me with weed to get her to be more agreeable."

"You two won't be leaving my grandbaby with them too often will you?"

"Ah, that would be a no. Lavender has already given them strict instructions on what they can and can't do around the baby." I tell him with a smirk.

He nods thoughtfully. "Yeah that's what I kind of figured. From what I hear, that woman is as straight laced as you can get. Her sister isn't too far off either."

I laugh. "Lav won't even curse. Hell, she keeps yelling at me every time that I do. She's determined to get me to stop completely before the baby is born."

He gives me a full blown smile and starts laughing. "How's that working out for you?"

I give him a sardonic smile. "How do you think it's going? Even words that aren't even that bad, she yells at me for. I swear, I can't catch a fucking break. She's got like super-sonic hearing or something. Every time I so much as mutter a word that she deems inappropriate, she hears me. I'm just waiting for her head to start spinning around."

Dad takes another sip and sits down next to me. "Son, I suggest you find a way to curb your mouth." He holds up a hand when I go to protest. "At least while she's pregnant. You do not want to be pissing off a pregnant woman. They can go from calm to grizzly bear in the blink of a damn eye."

"How the hell am I supposed to do that? I don't even think about it half the time. Some of them aren't actual curse words. I think that she's just making some of it up."

He shakes his head at me. "It doesn't matter. Don't be that dumb bastard who's sleeping on the couch because he pissed his woman off. You don't want that shit and I can guarantee, neither does your back. Just play by the rules that she sets out while her hormones are still playing a major role. Just keep your head down and follow the rules."

I lean back and rest my head against the wall. "And if I fail miserably?" I ask, because let's face it, I'm probably going to fail like it's my job.

He ponders my question for a moment. He looks around the garage. "Well then, I suggest that you find a space all of your own to go to. A little hideout if you will."

I look around the garage as well and think about how often Dad would be out here tinkering with this and that. "Is that why you were out here so much?"

He gives me a look that suggests I'm a moron. "Roc, there were four women in that house at one point. No shit that's why I was out here all the time. This was the safest place to be. Especially once your sisters turned into teenagers. I still have nightmares about that time period." He pretends to shiver at imaginary chills.

"So, I should clean out the garage for myself, is what you're saying." I could make that work. Winter will suck but I can always get a space heater or some shit.

Dad nods his head slowly while twirling his glass in his hands. "The garage or the basement. Just somewhere that you can go to stay out of her way. Especially when she's setting up the nursery. Just paint and put shit together and stay away from her unless she asks you for something. That room is going to be how she wants it and God help anyone who interrupts her."

I snort. "You're laying it on kind of thick old man."

He raises his eyebrow and takes a sip. "You'll see someday that I'm not just blowing smoke up your ass. Why don't you give your brother-in-laws a call and find out how much fun they had during that stage of your sister's pregnancies?"

I give him a smirk. "Come on now Dad. You know damn well that firefighters are big babies. They probably bitched more than Rachel and Amy ever did."

"Now, now son, just because firefighters are little bitches compared to police officers doesn't mean that those two bone heads didn't suffer." He chuckles.

It's been an ongoing fight over the years between those two and Dad and I. They're convinced that firefighters are better, while Dad and I try to explain to them how horribly wrong they are.

Needless to say, it's gotten a little loud a few times after a few too many beers. Mom and the girls have decided that we aren't allowed to bring anything up if we've been drinking anymore. One *accidental* punch and all of a sudden we're getting yelled at. It's not like anyone got shot.

Dad and I share a smile of superiority. "Fine, I'll figure out where to go to stay out of her way. I'm sure that it won't be that bad since Lav is such a sweetheart. She won't even curse, so I don't really see her flying off the deep end or anything."

"Don't ever underestimate the power of those hormones. And since Lavender is so sweet, you're probably going to have to worry about her crying at the drop of a dime. I'm telling you right now, make sure that you avoid commercials with abused animals. You just don't want the headache that one fifteen second commercial can cause."

I give him a grin. "No one watches anything with commercials anymore old man. Netflix and Prime video are the only way to do it these days. Didn't Kellie and I set that shit up for you and Mom?" I ask, because I know damn well that we did. I even got a slap to the nuts thanks to a pissy little sister.

He shrugs. "Eh, your mother doesn't like it. You know that she likes to watch *Wheel of Fortune* every night. It just doesn't make sense to keep switching over."

"You literally just press a button." I deadpan.

He waves a hand at me as he gets up to store away his bottle and glass. "That's more trouble than I feel like going through at night."

I look at him in disbelief. "Dad, it's one button. You just press one button. It even says Netflix, so it's not even like you have to figure out which one it is. You just press the button." I use my right hand to mimic pressing the button on my imaginary remote.

"Yeah, but then we have to look around and figure out where to go and what we want to watch. You know that we can never agree on something new. So, we spend the whole evening arguing over what to watch until it's time to go to bed. That's just a whole lot more trouble than it's worth if you ask me."

"You make marriage sound so fun and exciting. Please tell me more. You're making me want to find the nearest church and run to it." I drawl.

"No marriage is exciting all of the time. Anyone who tells you different is someone who gets cops showing up at their door a few times a week. I married the love of my life and best friend. But fact is that marriage is just two people asking each other what they want for dinner until they die." He says as he puts everything away and tidies up.

"I hope Lav and I have more fun than that." That shit sounds so boring.

Dad tosses my beer bottle in the garbage and puts his arm around my shoulders. We start making our way towards the exit. "That's life Rocco. Some times are exciting and others are boring. What makes it worth it, is who you wake up next to every morning."

We walk out the door and he squeezes my neck. "Now hurry your ass up before your mother kills us for being out here for too long." We both pick up the pace.

Today is the day...finally! Rocco and I finally get to find out the sex of our baby. I have been beyond excited for this day. I've barely slept in the past two days because I couldn't wait for today to get here. I know that it's either going to be a girl or a boy. It's not like I'm expecting to see an alien or anything.

But I can't wait to find out, that way we can start picking out names and decorating. I thought clothes shopping for me was fun, until I realized that I get to do it for a miniature human.

Baby clothes are the most adorable thing that I have ever seen in my life! I saw avocado pajamas and had to buy them. I figured those would be cute for a boy or a girl. I actually kind of wish that they sold them in adult sizes. I would definitely wear those.

These past few months have been the best and scariest time of my life. Scariest because against Rocco's advice, I googled everything that can go wrong in pregnancy. Let's just say, I made a colossal mistake - Rocco was nice enough not to say "I told you so" - and spent a very long time crying. I really should've listened to him.

In my defense, I really didn't expect there to be so many things that could go wrong. Google and webmd are two sites that I have banned myself from using without supervision. The pictures of preemies had me weeping for hours. Some of them were only one pound with translucent skin. My hormones just couldn't handle seeing that.

On the huge plus side, everything with Rocco has been amazing. Never in my wildest dreams did I ever think that I would find a man who is sweet, caring, protective and as loving as he is. I want to go back in time and slap myself upside my head for not talking to him sooner. I hate to think about how many months I wasted being a coward when we could've been together.

Every time I bring up how much I regret all those months, my sweet alphahole – Sage and Kay are bad influences – just smiles and tells me that he would deal with it all over again, if it meant that we ended up in the spot that we're in now. I really don't know what I would do without him anymore. As Sage likes to say, he's the calm to my neurotic.

Even right now, as we're driving to my doctor's appointment, he's calm and collected, just smiling and singing along with the radio. Me you ask? Well I'm more like a squirrel in traffic, who is barely missing getting hit by a car. My leg in jumping up and down and I can't stop fidgeting in my seat.

I look to my left and give a dirty look to the man at my side. "I don't understand how you are so calm right now. Aren't you excited to find out whether we'll be having a son or daughter?"

He looks over at me and gives me a quirk of his lips. He takes a few moments before answering. "I'm very excited to know if it's a girl or a boy. But we still have months and months left before the baby gets here. I think that I'm calm because it's still so far away."

This man is always beyond calm. I think that it would take a darn earthquake to rattle his cages. He's also been very selective about what he says. I swear, after that first dinner with his family, he's overly cautious about what he says to me.

He looks like he's afraid that I'm just going to fly off the handle at any moment. Men are just so very strange. He even asked me if he could turn the garage into a workout/den like place for himself so that he's not always in my way. It was nice that he asked me but it's his home too and he can do whatever he wants. Especially with the garage. The only thing I ever used it for was storage.

I roll my water bottle between my hands because for the life of me I can't sit still. "I know that." I sigh. "I guess that I am probably more excited than I should be. Especially with me having so much longer until my due date."

I lean my head against the window and watch the scenery outside. It's summer now and everything is in full bloom. I love this time of year but I could definitely do without this heat. I'm not even that big yet and the heat is killing me. I can only imagine how miserable women who are eight and nine months pregnant are.

Rocco drums his fingers against the steering wheel and looks over at me briefly. "Honey, I didn't mean that you shouldn't be excited. I think it's awesome how excited you are about the baby. I just meant that I won't get really excited until he or she is born and I'm holding them in my arms. Hell, I'll probably bawl like a baby myself that day."

"You've been doing so good with watching your language lately." I sigh loudly.

He groans at my statement. "Lav, hell is not even a bad word. I swear that you're just making some of this up."

I twist in my seat to look at him better and cross my arms. "It is too a bad word. You don't want our four or five- year-old child walking around saying that word...do you?"

"Obviously not but I'm a grown man Lav. I should be able to say what I want. I dealt with my mother bitching about my language while I was growing up. I feel like I should be able to do and say as I please."

"Huh." I huff out. I love him, I really do, but I have never met anyone who can press my buttons like he can.

He looks over and narrows his eyes at me. "Huh, what Lav?"

"I just think it's funny," I hear him mutter, *for the love of God,* but being nice, I choose to ignore it, "that you don't think that our children will repeat everything that their daddy says. You're a huge part of their life and will be the person that they look up to the most. Of course, they'll want to copy everything that you say. I see it all the time with the kids that I teach."

He's looking at me with a goofy grin that I can't understand. "Our children huh? Glad to know that we'll be having a few."

I point my finger at him. "Do not try to change the subject when I'm on a roll scolding you. I'm making a very good point right now."

"Anything you say dear." He singsongs at me.

I give a little growl at his response and his eyes widen. "It's not funny Rocco, I'm being extremely serious right now."

He nods his head and looks at me gravely. "I know honey. That growl was stuff that nightmares are made out of. I'm getting chills just thinking about it."

"You're really not funny." I huff and turn my head in the opposite direction so that I can look out the window again.

"If I'm not funny, then why are you smiling?"

"I'm not." I mutter, trying to keep my face very bland.

"You're not smiling right now?" He asks incredulously.

Thank goodness we are almost out of this truck. I can see my doctor's office just up ahead. "No."

"Must be gas then." He drawls.

I gasp and turn to look at him. "Rocco!" I hiss at the man at my side. "Do not talk like that. It's gross."

He starts to chuckle as he pulls into the parking lot and looks for a place to park. "Babe, it's a natural and normal part of life. There's no getting around it."

"It is not normal."

He parks the truck and blinks at me a few times. He then gets this mischievous look in his eyes that makes me uneasy. I've seen this look before directed at his sisters when he decides to torment them. "Are you trying to tell me that you don't fart sweetheart?"

I can feel the heat pouring off of my cheeks. "Rocco, I mean it. We are never, ever talking about this."

He holds his hands up like he's about to surrender. Unfortunately, I've gotten to know him really well these past few months and know that simply isn't the case. "What Lav? I'm just trying to find out if you do or not. If not, I want to make sure to ask the doctor about that. It can't be healthy for you and the baby to be keeping all of that in."

I narrow my eyes and try to give him a menacing growl, which truthfully a chihuahua makes a better one. "I mean it. You better not say a word about this conversation to anyone, or else."

His lips quirk at my statement. "Or else what sweetheart. You're about as threatening as a poodle."

I purse my lips and get inches away from his face. "Or else I'm going to do something really mean and horrific to you." I say with a smirk.

"Honey, I don't think that your brain could even come up with something mean. Let alone execute it properly."

"Well, okay, not me, but Sage and Kay could absolutely come up with something mean and carry it out for me."

"Yeah, that's probably the only way that would work out for you." He mumbles.

"You're being mean to me." I pout.

He gives me a big smile. "I'm not being mean sweetheart. I'm helping you forget about your nerves about finding out the sex of the baby. You haven't been fixated on it for the past few minutes while you've been yelling at me."

I open my mouth with a smart alec retort on the tip of my tongue, only to close it quickly when I realize that he's right. I have been nervous and fidgeting the past few minutes. Darn. "Thanks." I mumble petulantly. Good grief this pregnancy, and/or this man are turning me into one of my students.

He gives me a wide grin and unbuckles his seatbelt. "Don't mention it." He opens his door and turns back to look at me. "You ready to go in and see what we're having?"

My cheeks hurt with how big my smile gets. "Absolutely!" I do a little dance in my seat as Rocco walks over to open the door and help me out. His parents really taught him right. I haven't opened a door for myself in months.

When he gets to my side, he opens my door and holds out his right hand for me. "Alright gorgeous, let's get in there then."

I take his hand and he helps me out of the truck. We walk hand in hand into my doctor's office, which is mercifully empty. There is nothing worse than walking in, seeing it jam packed and knowing that you're going to be here for hours. That happened at one of my other appointments and Rocco is still complaining about it.

I go through the process of signing in and paying my copay. I turn around and grab Rocco's hand again, so that we can sit down, when I see a face that I wish to never see again. Just my luck that the one person that I never wish to see again would be sitting in the waiting room.

Derrick and his very pregnant wife, - seriously, how many children do they have now – are sitting in the back corner of the room. How is this even possible? I know that we live in a small town, but come on, it isn't this darn small. He's sitting looking down at his phone and to my immense joy, I realize that the only thing that I feel for him is loathing.

Looking back on the relationship now, I realize how poorly he truly treated me and that I deserved so much better than him. Rocco has shown me with every kiss, smile, hug, compliment and joke, what a real relationship with a good man should be. I mean, my crazy, sweet man even picks up a chocolate milkshake for me almost daily without me asking, because he knows how much I love them.

I now see how one sided my relationship with Derrick really was. But at the time, it was devastating to find out that he had been cheating on me, with the woman sitting here, and that he was going to live happily ever after with someone else. Hindsight is always twenty/twenty I suppose, because now I wake up every morning thanking God that he is no longer in my life.

And it most definitely means that I have no urge to ever see him again. It's funny how you can block out all of the mean and spiteful things that someone has done and said to you, until they all come rushing back. Standing here looking at Derrick, I can suddenly recall every vile thing that he ever said and or did to me.

"You okay sweetheart?" Rocco asks while standing next to me caressing my back.

I look up and give him a pained smile. His question brought the attention of Derrick along with it. Before I can respond to Rocco, I'm interrupted by a voice that now sounds like nails on a chalkboard to me.

"What in the hell are you doing here?" Derrick asks none too nicely.

Rocco protectively steps in front of me. I can feel his muscles bunching under my hands. I've never seen Rocco angry, most of the other guys never have either, except for JJ.

He was the one who told me that Rocco is mellow until you truly piss him off. Once that happens, it's best to stay out of his way. Something about being Irish and Italian. I didn't really pay much attention to what JJ said at the time. I'm now regretting that bad decision.

"Who do you think that you're talking to like that?" Rocco asks in a voice that's calm, eerily so.

I can see Derrick about to speak before he catches the obvious aggression that's coming off of Rocco in waves. Compared to Derrick, Rocco's a giant wall of muscle. I probably shouldn't be as smug as I'm feeling right now, but oh well, I'm allowed to be petty sometimes too.

"Ah, I didn't mean it like that." He backpedals like a sniveling fool. Oh gee, look at me today, Sage would be so proud. "I was just surprised to see Lavender, that's all."

"Right." Rocco growls. That should not make certain bits all tingly.

"I thought that you said that you weren't able to have children?" Derrick asks like a huge dope.

I step forward a little and find a chair to walk to – as far away from those two as possible – and take a seat. I give them a small smirk. "Apparently, I can with the right man." I shrug casually, so very proud of myself for finally standing up to him, even if it's a few years too late to really matter.

Rocco snorts while taking a seat next to me. When I look over at him, he gives me a wink and settles in. I don't miss the fact that he's sat himself in between me and Derrick. I need to remember to thank him properly later.

"Congratulations." Derricks wife Lilly – I know, he has a weird thing for women named like flowers – says, sounding genuine.

"Thank you." I give her a small smile. I don't harbor any ill feelings towards her. I even heard that Derrick had lied to her about our relationship. It's not her fault that he's a jerk.

We all remain quiet after that and it could not be any more awkward in here. Derrick keeps looking over at us with a sneer on his face. Lilly appears to be trying to disappear into her chair. I'm trying to pretend that they aren't here.

And Rocco...well, he appears to be sleeping. He's stretched his long body out. He has his legs crossed, arms crossed against his chest and his head is resting against the back of his chair with his eyes closed. I would believe that he was asleep if it wasn't for his hand flexing and unflexing like he's trying to mentally talk himself out of something.

I think even the women who work here have caught onto the vibe in the room because they keep looking between the four of us with wide, curious eyes. And to think that just an hour ago, I was beyond happy and excited for today. Now all I want to do is get the heck out of here. I swear Derrick is the biggest black cloud that has ever walked the earth.

Mercifully, they're called into the room fairly quickly. Rocco opens his eyes the minute the door closes behind them. I look up and give him a smirk, that causes him to raise his eyebrows.

"I knew that you weren't sleeping." I giggle.

He looks down and gives me – as his mother calls it – his charming, innocent little boy smile. Let me tell you, there is absolutely nothing innocent about it. That smile of his is lethal to my out of control hormones.

"I was just pretending that I was in a happy place." He tells me, causing me to frown.

I lean over and place my hand on top of his arm. "Why would you have to do that?"

"Because if I didn't, I was going to walk over and kick the living shit out of your scumbag ex." He says merrily before placing a kiss to the top of my head. "I figured that you wouldn't be happy about that, so, I closed my eyes and decided to think happy thoughts."

I nod slowly. "You're right, I would've been upset about that." He's correct about that. But it's sweet that he was thinking happy thoughts. I smile up at him. "What were you thinking about?"

He looks down at me with a megawatt smile. "Damon pushing him in front of a car."

I cough into my hand as I choke on my saliva. Rocco ever so helpfully pats me on the back. "That was not even close to what I was expecting you to say." I purse my lips.

He looks at me carefully before just shrugging. "It was either day dream about it, or do it. I chose the option that wouldn't land me in a cell with you being mad at me."

"It's hard to believe some days that you guys are all police officers."

He gets a thoughtful expression on his handsome face and rubs his stubble covered chin with his right hand. "You're not the first person to say something along those lines. And you most likely won't be the least either."

I give him a look that I'm sure conveys how crazy that statement was. "You don't have any problem at all with that huh? None, what-so-ever?"

"I used to." He states while nodding his head. "But after a while, I learned to just go with the flow. It makes things easier to deal with in the long run."

"I feel like that's not something that you should just go along with." I say carefully.

"Probably not." He agrees. "But it's a little too late now. Might as well just make the best of it."

"How do you go about making the best out of it?" I ask genuinely curious. I should most likely be more appalled by this conversation than I am.

"By realizing that I have a group of men at my back who would be more than willing to help me dump that shithead's body if anything ever happened to him."

"Again, not a proper thing for a police officer to say." I sigh knowing that I'm not going to get anywhere with this conversation.

They are all absolutely some of the best men that I have ever met. They really are caring, generous, protective and sweet. At the same time however, they are also crazy, sneaky and just plain nuts. I understand that they do things because they are all completely overprotective, but good grief, someone got hit by a car and all they do is joke about it!

"I feel like this is one of those things that you and I are really never going to see eye to eye on, honey." He tells me while scratching the side of his head.

"Probably not sweetie." My smile only slightly looks like a grimace, I'm sure.

"Lavender." Is called from the doorway.

I look over and smile at the nurse. "Right here."

She gives me a bright smile and waves a hand, motioning for us to follow her. "Come on back to ultrasound."

Rocco and I look at each other and we both widen our eyes at the same time. This is it! We finally get to know what we're having. I grab his hand and he squeezes mine, before helping me stand up.

We follow the nurse down the hall, hand in hand. She leads us to the ultrasound room, where the technician is sitting and waiting for us. The technician is probably in her late twenties and is cute as a button. She has the most awesome unicorn scrubs on that I've ever seen.

"I love your scrubs!" I gush, because... hello, unicorns!

She gives me a bright smile. "Thank you! I just got them the other day. When I saw them, I knew that they were coming home with me." She rubs her hands together excitedly. "So, ya'll ready to see what you're having?"

Rocco snorts loudly. "This one's," he tilts his head in my direction, "been ready since we found out that she was pregnant."

I give him a shove that was basically the equivalent of a toddler pushing a giant. "I haven't been that bad."

His eyes widen comically, causing the technician to giggle. "You haven't slept in two days! Who are you trying to lie to with your "*I haven't been that bad*" nonsense?"

I can feel my face go red. "I wasn't that bad." I mutter. "And don't act like you haven't been the tiniest bit excited too." I huff.

He nods slowly. "Yeah, but at least I slept." He drawls annoyingly.

I look up at him and give him a sweet smile. "If my waking up is keeping you up, you can always sleep on the couch to ensure that you get a restful night's sleep."

We hear a cough that sounds suspiciously like a laugh coming from the technician that we both ignore.

His eyes narrow at me. "You've been spending way too much time with Declan and your sister. They're trying to turn you as evil as they are." He moans like a loon.

I roll my eyes at the big goofball. "Stop being such a baby."

"Speaking of babies, hop on up here." The technician pats the table. "Just lift your shirt and we'll get started."

I do as instructed and get up on the table and lie down. I lift my shirt, which thanks to my very large belly already, is a maternity shirt and place it right below my breasts.

"This might be a little cold." She warns before squirting a large glob of jelly on my stomach.

I jump when it makes contact with my skin, because cold isn't a good enough description of how freezing this stuff is. "Wow, you weren't kidding about it being cold."

She gives me a grimace while clicking a bunch of stuff on the screen. "Yeah, sorry about that. We normally have a bottle warmer, but it broke a few days ago and we haven't gotten a new one yet."

Rocco is standing over me looking like a worried mother hen. "Are you okay sweetheart?"

I give him a bright smile and grab his hand. "I'm good honey. Just getting really excited again." I refuse to let Derrick's presence ruin any more of my life.

The technician places the wand on my stomach and starts moving it around. The first thing we hear is the whooshing sound from the baby's heart. You never realize how a simple sound can make everything in the world better. That heartbeat means that are baby is alive and well. And just like clockwork, cue the waterworks.

Poor Rocco looks so alarmed that I would laugh if I could. "Baby, what's wrong? Is she hurting you? We can tell her to stop." He rambles.

I swipe my fingers under my eyes and smile up at the sweet man by my side. "I'm fine, I promise. These are happy tears, I swear it. I'm just so happy to hear the baby's heartbeat, that's all. After reading about all the bad stuff that can happen, I'm just a little emotional about it."

"Ah, okay, if you're sure that you're alright?" This poor guy.

"I promise, only happy tears." I giggle at the look on his face. I can tell that he wants to believe me but the way he's squeezing my hand says differently.

I look at the technician and see her clicking things on the screen. She looks at me and gives me a smile when she catches me staring at her like a weirdo. "I'm just taking a few measurements to make sure that the baby is the size that it should be. After that, we can get on with seeing if the baby will be shy or is letting it all hang out today."

"Wait, so we might not be able to find out what the baby is today?" Rocco asks her with a frown on that handsome scruffy face of his.

She winces a bit. "It really depends on the baby truthfully. You wouldn't believe how many little ones have their legs crossed or just refuse to move at all. Some of them are very stubborn and don't like being disturbed." She chuckles.

Rocco has my hand in a death grip. Geez, what happened to mister, *"I probably won't get excited until the baby is born"*? I chuckle mentally.

"So, what would happen if we can't find out today? Do we get to come back tomorrow or something?" He asks with such an earnest look on his face. Poor guy is going to be crushed if we don't find out today.

"Unfortunately, no. You would have to wait until her next scan to find out. Or you could go to an imaging place. They actually have places specifically to find out the gender of the baby."

"Seriously?" I ask. "They have places just for that reason?" That's just crazy.

"Yup." She says while popping the P. "Let me tell you, those places are absolute goldmines. They charge like a hundred dollars for the scan and everything else like a picture and stuff is even more. Whoever came up with the idea is a genius."

"Who would actually waste money on all of that?" I mean really, what a waste.

Rocco is giving me a wide-eyed look while blinking furiously. "What do you mean, *who would actually waste money on that*? We will be if we can't find out today."

Now it's my turn to blink up at him. Is he for real right now? "Rocco, we are not wasting money on something like that. We have so many better uses for our money instead of wasting it on that."

"It wouldn't be a waste." He defends with his arms crossed over his well-defined chest. "It would make us happy. Therefore, it's not a waste."

"There are plenty of things that make me happy that I will not spend money on. Especially money that is better spent on stuff for this baby. Not spending an insane amount on getting a scan that I have done in this office for free thanks to my insurance. So, no we will not be doing that." I cross my arms, mimicking – poorly – his pose.

"Oh yes we are."

I narrow my eyes at the man getting on my nerves. "Oh really? And how do you plan on doing that without the one who's pregnant?" I ask in a saccharine voice.

He gives me an obnoxious smirk. "You act like you aren't small enough for me to just pick up and take you with me."

"I dare you." I growl. Sheesh, the man can get on my last nerve.

We hear a snort and I flush bright red just now remembering that the poor woman is in the room with us as we're bickering.

"None of that will be necessary because your little one is a total showoff." She giggles. "So, Mom and Dad, are you ready to find out what you're having?" She asks while moving the wand around my stomach some more.

Rocco and I both look at each other and smile, completely forgetting that we were just arguing a moment ago. I grab his hand again and squeeze it. "You ready to find out Daddy?"

He gives me his megawatt smile and bends down, placing a kiss on the top of my head. "I'm game if you are." He mumbles into my hair.

I look over at the woman and give her a big smile. "We are more than ready to find out what this little one is."

She smiles up at us brightly. "Congratulations, Mom and Dad, you are having a little boy with no modesty."

A boy! It's a boy!

Hours later and I still can't contain my excitement. We're having a son and I couldn't be any more fucking stoked if I tried. Don't get me wrong, I would've been happy if it was a girl too. But I just don't think that I could mentally handle having a girl first.

I know that it sounds sexist, but fuck it. There is so much more shit that you have to worry about when you have a girl, compared to having a boy. Just the thought of a teenage girl dating and being out on her own is enough to drive me to the brink. Hell, I'm pretty sure that my nieces are starting to age me prematurely. So, having my own daughter? Forget about it, I'd look like I'm eighty at the age of forty.

Plus, I'll get to do a bunch of fun stuff with him. Teaching him how to play catch, how to work on cars, taking him fishing and teaching him how to shoot a gun and throw a punch in case he has a little sister. You know, all the important things in life.

"Why do you have a creepy smile on your face?" Lavender asks from the passenger seat of my truck.

We went straight to my parent's house after the doctor's appointment to tell them the good news. To say that they were happy is an understatement. My mother started bawling her eyes out, causing everyone else who was there - my entire family – to start crying along with her.

"I was just thinking about the scene at my parent's house." I lie easily. There is no way that I'm telling her that I'm already planning out some more children.

Her eyes widen and she blows out a big breath. "That was something, that's for sure. Your mother is sweet but has a bad case of baby fever."

I look over at her briefly while making sure that I don't get us into an accident before we make it to Sage's. "What do you mean?"

She snorts like a cute little piglet. "She tried convincing me that I don't really need to take any maternity leave from my job. And that was after she gave me a death glare when I brought up daycare. I swear, for a moment, I thought that she was going to stab me."

I grimace knowing exactly how my mother probably reacted to that. "You actually said the word daycare to her?"

Lav bangs the back of her head against the headrest. Once she's done, she rolls her head to the side to look at me. "I didn't think that she would freak out about it the way that she did."

"Honey, she's watched all of my sisters' kids. Didn't you think that she might do the same for us?" I ask gently, no need to piss off a sleeping bear.

"Sure." She shrugs sheepishly. "But I didn't want to be presumptuous. I also figured that I would be giving her an out in case she just wanted to enjoy her retirement instead of having to take care of another child." She says quietly.

I use my right hand to grab her left. I bring it up to my mouth and plant a kiss on her soft palm. "Sweetheart, that was very thoughtful but my mom honestly lives for this. She's never happier than when she's taking care of one or all of the kids. Trust me when I say that nothing in this world would make her happier than for us to have her watch the little guy while we're at work."

She rolls her pretty eyes at me. "Yeah, I get that now." She chuckles. "She really drove her point home when she tried to tell me that I really only need a week or two off after giving birth before I should be okay to go back to work."

"Yeah, that sounds about right when it comes to her and babies, especially her grandbabies." I muse out loud.

"At least we don't have to worry about paying those astronomical daycare prices." She sighs. "Can you believe that they charge you a darn mortgage payment for one child a month?" She says animatedly. "I can't even imagine what people with more than one child do. They're working basically just to send their child to daycare. It's absolutely absurd that those places charge so much."

I raise my eyebrow at her little rant. "You okay honey?"

She huffs and crosses her arms. "Yes, I'm fine. I was just looking up some places just in case the other day and could not believe what I saw. It's incredible how much they charge people. I guess I'm just a little bit more upset about it than I thought. It just seems so unfair to people who live paycheck to paycheck, you know?"

I nod my head because I wholeheartedly agree with her. "Yeah baby, I get it and agree. That's why everyone in my family knows how much of a blessing my mother is. She may be nuts when it comes to babies but it's her love of them that saves all of our wallets."

"You make her sound like some crazy baby kidnapper or something." She giggles.

"Lav, you literally just told me, that my mother just tried to convince you to go back to work, two weeks after giving birth. If that doesn't scream baby crazy, I don't know what does."

She purses her luscious lips and gives a tiny grimace. "Okay, you have a point. She definitely is a little bit beyond where other grandmothers are when it comes to their grandchildren."

"Look at it this way, we'll always be able to have a date night. Granted it'll probably be because she refused to give him up for the night. But we can always look on the bright side."

Lav gives me a horrified look. "Would she actually do that? Refuse to give him back to us?"

"Of course not." I lie through my teeth. My mother is the biggest baby hog that the world has ever seen. I have no doubt that she would try to refuse to let us take him home so that she could cuddle with him more. "I was just kidding babe."

She lets out a huge sigh of relief. "Okay, that's good." We'll just cross that bridge when we get to it.

We're quiet for the rest of the drive to Sage and JJ's, which isn't very long since we live in such a small town. They live on a quaint street with another matching house. The perfect little suburban home.

As I pull up in front of the house, I can see that Kayla's SUV is here, meaning that she, Marc and their brood are inside as well. I also see Danny's truck here parked at the curb too. "Looks like a packed house tonight." I say while tilting my head for Lav to see the car.

She just gives me a smile and shrugs. "Makes it easier telling people what we're having if they're all already here."

She unbuckles her seatbelt but waits for me to get out and come around to help her out. That definitely seemed to take her a while to get used to. I open her door, grab her hips and lift her out of the truck. If she accidentally slides down my body while I place her on the ground...so be it. Though, judging by the tiny scowl she has on her beautiful face, I'm guessing she's caught onto how that accidentally happens each time.

"Can you not do that before we're about to go in and see a bunch of our friends?" She hisses like a little kitten.

I make sure to put my game – confused – face on. "Do what sweetheart?"

Her eyes turn into tiny slits while looking up at me. She takes her index finger and jabs it into my sternum. "Do not play dumb with me Rocco. You may be able to fool everyone else but I know that you're an incredibly intelligent man. So, knock it off."

With that parting remark, she turns on her heel and storms up to her sister's front door. Have I ever mentioned how adorable she is when she's huffing and puffing. I know, I'm probably going to hell. But the way I see it, is I'm already going there for a bunch of other shit anyway, so I might as well enjoy my life.

I make sure to catch up to her before anyone answers the door. She gives me a cute growl when I place my arms around her. "Are you going to be pissy the rest of the night?" I ask while nuzzling the side of her neck with the scruff on my chin. I'm rewarded with the small giggle that I was after.

"Cut it out." She tries and fails miserably to shoulder me away from her. "I'm still mad at you and I plan to stay that way for a good long while."

"We both know that you can never stay mad at me." I croon. "You enjoy snuggling up to me too much. What would you do without my sexy body anymore?"

She looks back at me with a very Sage-like look in her eyes. "Find a sexy fire fighter?"

Of course JJ takes that moment to open the fucking door. He doesn't pretend not to laugh very well either.

I glare at my entire world. "Take that back." I growl.

She blinks up at me with innocent doe eyes that aren't fooling me in the slightest. "What honey? You asked me a question and I answered it, easy peasy." She shrugs and then looks over at the person not even pretending that he's not standing there listening to every word.

"Hi JJ." She says sweetly as she places a kiss on his cheek before entering the house.

"Hey Lav." He chuckles and lets her pass him, so that she can go in and find her horrible influence of a sister.

My best friend and surrogate older brother looks at me with a shit eating grin on his face that I want to knock off. "So, how's it going?"

"Shut up." I mumble.

"That's gotta sting buddy. Everyone knows that fire fighters are second best. Damn, she'd rather have the B team than you." He laughs like a jackass at his own dumb joke.

Just wonderful, I see Marc and Danny making their way over. I give JJ a glare. "Can I come in, or am I supposed to stand here all night?"

He clucks his tongue at me but gets out of my way and lets me enter. "Someone's a little cranky tonight."

"Who's cranky?" The tall, nosey fucker asks.

I say, "No one," at the exact same time that JJ says, "Rocco."

"What's wrong? Skip naptime?" Marc asks while the other two fools chuckle.

"It's just been a long day, that's all."

"Lav said that she would take a firefighter over him."

"She didn't say it like that." I defend with my arms crossed.

"I feel your pain man." Marc sympathizes. "Kay once told me that she liked looking at pictures of fire fighters on her Instagram."

"How'd you get her to stop?" Danny questions.

Marc looks at him with the blank look that he uses when he's done something bad. "I didn't." He states casually...too casually.

I purse my lips and know that I'll probably regret asking. "Nothing? She didn't stop looking at that shit?"

"I didn't say that."

He shakes his head.

I decide to lean back against the wall, since it doesn't seem like we're going to be moving from the foyer anytime soon.

"So, what are you saying exactly?" JJ asks giving him a dubious look.

Anyone who has ever met Marc, knows that there is absolutely no way in hell that he just left it alone. No chance of him having Kay look at other men, especially fire fighters.

"All I'm saying is, that I didn't have to ask her to do anything because somehow all those accounts got deleted and blocked from her feed."

"And you had nothing to do with that happening?" JJ drawls in disbelief. I look over at Danny and can see that he isn't buying that for a minute either.

"You know that I'm not tech savvy." Marc plainly states.

I give JJ a head tilt, because Marc isn't lying. He doesn't do any social media or anything like that. He probably wouldn't be able to figure out how to do it.

"Who did you blackmail into doing it for you?" I ask because Lord help me, but I really need to know who he's blackmailed now. Poor Declan will never live down being an ugly hooker.

He gives the three of us his winning smile. "It's honestly amazing how helpful teenage girls are when you say the word *Sephora.*"

"Clever. They would definitely be the ones to go to for all that shit." Danny states with approval shining in his eyes.

"Anyway," JJ side-eyes Marc before looking over at me. "How did the doctor's appointment go today?"

I can feel my smile get huge. "We're having a little guy who likes to let it all hang out."

JJ's face lights up. "No shit? Us too, we just found out yesterday."

"Congrats brother." I say before we hug and slap each other a few times on the back.

The other two give us a round of congratulations as well. We all turn our heads when we hear the women screaming in the kitchen.

"I guess they know as well now." Marc chuckles.

Abby and Logan come walking out of the kitchen with their hands over their ears, with Max following closely behind.

"Uncle Rocco!" Abby screeches when she sees me. She runs full blast at me and jumps into my arms. I catch her just in time before she hits my nuts. "Guess what?" She asks while smooshing my face in between her tiny hands.

"What's up pretty girl?" I say as best as I can with her pushing my lips together.

"Aunt Sage and aunt Lavender are both having baby boys!" She whispers like she's telling me the world's biggest secret.

I, of course, widen my eyes in shock appropriately. "Really?" I gasp. "How do you know?"

She rolls her eyes like the gigantic ball of sass that she is. "Duh. Didn't you just hear them screaming?"

"That's what that was?"

"Yes." She nods her head with wide eyes.

"Should we go see?" I ask her in a whisper.

"Yeah, let's go."

I carry her into the kitchen with everyone else trailing behind us. When I walk in, I see Sage and Lav jumping up and down hugging each other.

"Are you guys allowed to do that while pregnant? It doesn't seem very safe." I ask, because seriously, that can't be healthy for the babies.

I hear a snort off to my side and see Kayla sitting at the table. She gives me a smirk when she sees me. "They're perfectly fine. Believe it or not, they could even do crossfit until like their eight month or something. You men are ridiculous when it comes to pregnancy."

"We're not ridiculous." The four of us say in unison.

"Uh-huh." She mutters like taking a sip of what appears to be iced tea.

Max walks into the room excitedly. "Mom, guess what I nudist?"

We all blink at him a few times. You can see Kayla biting back a smile. "Do you mean noticed, sweetie?"

He nods his head. "That's what I said, nudist."

She puffs out her cheeks while the rest of us snicker quietly. "Right, sure. So, what did you notice?"

"That aunt Lavender's ex-boyfriend keeps driving by the house really slowly. He keeps looking at the windows."

It takes us all a moment to process what he's just said, but damn, I was not expecting that shit.

Marc kneels down to his level. "You saw Derrick driving by this house, slowly...just now?"

Max nods his head. "Yep. But I gave him the finger like you taught me to do to douchebags. He looked mad and then drove away really quickly."

There is so much to process from that one sentence.

"Marc?" Kay asks in a sweet voice that doesn't match the daggers shooting out of her eyes.

Marc looks back at his wife with what can only be described as trepidation. "Yeah, darlin'?"

"What is he talking about?" She has the brightest and fakest smile on her face that I have ever seen.

"Apparently, Lavender's ex is being a creeper and driving by for some reason."

Got to give it to him. The man can definitely think on his feet. The rest of us just snigger quietly.

If looks could kill, Marc would be dead. I wouldn't put it past Kay to be mentally drowning him right now. "You know damn well that's not what I meant?"

"Are you sure? Because it seems like that's the most pressing issue at the moment."

Even from across the kitchen I can see her eye twitching a bit. This fool is going to die tonight, for sure. "This discussion isn't over." She growls at him.

"What discussion?" He blinks innocently at her. He's either really brave or really dumb. I'm not sure which right now.

"I'm really going to look the other way when your sister decides to stab you at some point."

"Well that's just mean and uncalled for." He sniffs.

It's taking everything I have to keep a straight face. Kay is turning a shade of red that I've only ever seen on a cooked lobster before. I think that she might be the one stabbing him soon.

"As much as I love seeing Kay mentally planning ways to off Marc, can we get back to my sister's scummy ex please?" Sage drawls from where she's standing by the sink.

"I can't believe that we're seeing him again." Lav mutters more to herself but we all hear it.

Sage's head whips around in her direction. "What do you mean seeing him again? Why the hell has that sack of shit been anywhere near you?" She has her hands on her hips and is glaring at her sister.

Lav gives a big sigh. "Him and Lilly go to the same doctor that I do."

"Jesus! That chick is pregnant again? What, are they trying for a damn football team now?" Kay asks incredulously.

"Yeah, and they were sitting in the waiting room when we walked in. He was rude and it was awkward, but I just can't fathom why he would be driving past your house." Lav says thoughtfully.

Marc stands up and looks at JJ, Danny and I with an unsettling gleam in his eyes. You know that type of gleam that nothing good ever comes from? He's got that going on in spades. I see JJ physically deflate, like he knows that there is no stopping whatever is about to happen. The only thing he can do is supervise to make sure that it doesn't go sideways.

"We can always go wait in the garage and ask him when he comes around again." Marc says with too much enthusiasm.

"You do realize that you're an officer of the law, right?" JJ questions him.

"Huh, and here I was thinking that I was a male model." Marc replies.

We hear a gag and look at Sage. "I think that I just threw up in my mouth."

We ignore the girls giggles and continue staring at the world's worst ring leader.

"How are you going to ask a dude in a car some questions?" Danny asks. It's a valid question really. It's not like Derrick is on foot or anything.

The smile that comes across Marc's face is somewhat chilling. "Don't worry about it. You just leave that up to me."

"This isn't going to end well." Kay mutters.

"Does it ever end well when he's involved?" Sage replies while grabbing her glass of iced tea. "But look on the bright side. You'll have the bed all to yourself while he's in jail."

Marc covers his heart with both of his hands and stumbles backwards making the kids - who we all seemed to have forgotten about – laugh. "Your lack of faith in me hurts my feelings."

"I'm sure that you'll get over it."

"So, we doing this or what?" Danny asks while jumping on the balls of his feet and cracking his neck and knuckles.

Marc looks on with a smile and swipes his thumb in Danny's direction. "I like him."

"I'm so glad that you're making a new friend." JJ deadpans. "But how about we just get this over with and see if we can find out what he wants?"

"My guess is a beat down since he's driving by here. Especially since the last time I saw him, I told him that I would do just that if he ever came near the three girls again." Danny says with a smile creepy enough to match Marc's.

This is one of those moments that I know that I should be the sane and rational one in the group. I know damn well that I should talk these two fools out of whatever it is that they're planning on doing. I understand that's what I should be doing.

But, as much as I know that I should be the voice of reason, I just can't force any words out of my mouth to stop them. Honestly, the only thing I want to know is what the plan is.

"I'll be in the garage." Marc states before giving Kay a quick kiss and walking out, with Danny following right behind him.

The kids try to follow him before Kay puts a stop to it. "Don't even think about it. You three go find the girls and Lexi and sit in there with them."

All three whine but do as she says, with minimal grumbling about life not being fair.

Lavender is looking at me with a worried look while biting that full pink bottom lip of hers. "You're not going to let him do anything to get in trouble over...right?"

"Of course not honey." I say.

The three traitors all snort...loudly. I give them a glare that does nothing. "Please, he's probably going to help them with joy." Sage tells her.

"You don't know that." I defend. I mean, I could be the good one in the group today. I'm not going to be but she doesn't know that for sure.

"Rocco, you know damn well that you could've stopped my foolish husband before the idea fully formed in his head. You know that bad things happen when he starts plotting. But you made absolutely no effort to stop him. That means that you plan on going along with whatever stupidity that he comes up with."

"Kay's right you know." JJ chimes in. "You looked downright happy at his proclamation."

I scoff at the man at my side. "You're his superior. You could've fucking put a stop to it easily. You stood there and didn't say a single word to deter him." I cross my arms and glare at him.

JJ sighs and rubs his temples. "I'm old, tired and about to have a newborn again. I just don't have any fucks left in me to stop him. As long as no one ends up dead, I just don't give a shit anymore."

The girls and I just silently stare at him. "You're such a good role model for all the kids." Sage says with sarcasm dripping from every word.

He gives her a side-eyed look. "Out of the entire group of us, I'm probably the only one that is."

"I'm not that bad." I mumble, not entirely offended though.

He looks over at me with a raised eyebrow. "You aren't that good, especially right now, either."

"Touché." I concede.

JJ grabs me by the neck like a mother would grab her pups. "If you'll excuse us ladies. We have to go make sure nothing irreversible happens."

With that he drags us out to the garage where we see Marc and Danny having a very animated conversation.

This is probably not going to go well. But fuck it, you only live once.

Twenty Something Minutes Later:

I might've been a little too hasty with my fuck it earlier. Although, I can't say that I fully regret how things ended up. And hey, on the plus side, everyone is still very much alive! I really should look into getting some normal and sane friends. Maybe ones who work in an office or something equally boring.

Everyone is alive but Derrick is definitely worse for the wear. I also don't know why Marc thought that it would be a great idea to tie him to a chair in the middle of the fucking garage. JJ is pacing around like a caged animal and I can't say that I blame him. This is his house after all and he's technically our boss.

Marc's bright idea on getting Derrick to stop and get out of the car? Marc walked directly in front of the car and almost got hit. When Derrick got out to see if he was okay, Danny came up behind him and dragged him into the garage. It all happened so quickly that JJ and I really didn't have much time to react. Not that I was going to stop them, but still, it was fast.

I wonder if other cops are as shitty as we are. Don't get me wrong, when I'm on duty, I am all about the law. But really, that should still apply more when I'm off duty. I just don't have the slightest inkling to make this stop right now. But we can't be the only police officers who are like this...right? Nah, there's probably a huge amount out there like us.

JJ's giving me a funny look. "What the hell do you keep nodding your head about?" He asks me in a hushed whisper.

I look at him and give him a smile. "Just thinking about some positive reaffirmations."

JJ's lips purse and he opens and closes his mouth a few times. He rubs his hands over his eyes. "I'm too old for this shit and all of you. I swear, you assholes have aged me more than Paige ever has."

"Love you too buddy." I smirk.

"Can we just get on with this shitshow already?" He asks in a defeated tone.

"Patience is a virtue." Marc says while looking over various tools.

"What are you looking for?" I ask because now I realize that Danny has been looking around as well.

"A sledgehammer or a crowbar." Marc mutters distractedly.

"For what?" JJ asks with a sudden twitch appearing in his jaw.

Marc blanks his face. "No reason."

The shit stain that is Lavender's ex finally catches onto why Marc would want that stuff and starts thrashing about in his chair. Unfortunately for him, he's in there very securely.

"What do you want?" He sobs like a pansy. Jesus we haven't even done anything to him and he's crying like a little bitch. The teenage girls handle their shit better.

Marc gives him a smile that even causes chills to run down my spine. "We just want to ask you a few questions." His voice is high and chipper. The fucker really can be a creepy bastard at times.

"About what?" Derrick keeps looking between the four of us, like he isn't sure who to focus his attention on.

"We just want to know why you keep driving past here. That's all. Just some friendly question and answers. Then you can be on your way." Marc says while palming a crowbar.

If this guy pisses or shits himself, I am not cleaning up the mess.

"I saw Lavender today and I was just wondering how she's doing and I remembered that her sister lives here. That's all. I just wanted to check up on her."

Marc takes a seat on a rolling stool directly in front of Derrick. He still towers over him, causing the other man to shrink back in his seat. I'm not going to lie. This is the most enjoyable thing that I've watched in a long time.

"See, I just don't buy that man. You don't toss a woman aside years ago and then decide to check up on her. I feel like you're trying to give me a line of bull and I just really don't like it."

"That's all that I was doing. And you can't tie me up like this. Do you have any idea who my father-in-law is? I'll make sure he has your badges for this." He hisses.

"Have our badges for what? You almost hit me with your car and then started yelling at us all. We even have a celebrity witness that says you were verbally aggressive towards us for no reason."

"You have me tied to a chair!" He screeches.

Marc chuckles darkly. "Who's going to believe you over three police officers and a home-grown golden boy? Everyone is going to think that you're crazy. Then add in the fact that you were driving past your ex's sister's house and well...hmm." Marc taps his finger to his lips. "That's not going to look too good to your wife and in-laws, now is it?"

Derrick remains quiet but doesn't try to conceal the hatred in his eyes. Damn, Marc really is good at shit like this.

Danny steps forward with a wicked grin on his face. "Remember what I told you would happen if you ever came near any of them again?"

His eyes bulge and I can't keep myself from chuckling. This turned out to be a really great day.

I look over at the man that I love more than life and I'm pretty sure that I'm going to kill him. Why would I want to kill the father of my unborn – he better decide to get out of my belly soon – child? Because this dope has just informed me that we have plans to meet everyone for dinner in less than an hour.

I am a million – nine – months pregnant. I can't even pee in under an hour these days. I haven't seen my feet in months, so I'm not even entirely sure that I'm wearing matching socks.

Nothing fits because apparently we're having a gigantic baby. He's so big that people actually keep asking me if I have gestational diabetes. I seriously can barely fit into anything other than dresses that look like mumus and extremely stretchy leggings. I look like a darn beached whale.

And now he tells me that he forgot to mention our dinner plans a week ago! A week he's known about this!

"Baby, stop staring at me like that. You look beautiful already. All you have to do is just put on some shoes and we can leave." The walking dead tells me.

Yeah, that's one thing about this pregnancy that I'm really enjoying, I seem to have a snarky side. I'm no Sage or Kay, but I've been entertaining myself a bit.

I sigh and pinch the bridge of my nose. I shut my eyes and count to ten so that I don't say something that I'll regret when I'm not hormonal and homicidal. "Rocco," I say through extremely gritted teeth. "I need to change, do my hair and put on makeup. That would take not pregnant me more than an hour. Shamu me will take at least two hours just to squeeze myself into some sort of top."

He starts banging his head with the remote. Right, because I'm the one causing an issue here. "Babe, I love you, I really do but you are acting insane. Why in the hell would it take you two hours to get ready? All you have to do is put some damn shoes on. You're already dressed!"

"Not in cute clothes Rocco!" I yell back. "I'm wearing comfy clothes."

He blinks repeatedly at me. "Isn't that what you want? You complain all the damn time about how uncomfortable you are. Shouldn't you want to wear comfy clothes when going out to dinner?"

I snort and put my hands on my freakishly large hips. "No, you wear cute clothes when going out with a group of friends. You never wear comfy clothes. I don't want people to think I'm homeless!"

He throws his arms up in the air. "How are you homeless? You're wearing your stretchy pants and a t-shirt. You look like every other woman on the fucking planet."

I narrow my eyes at this jerk. "Do not take that tone with me and watch your language, the baby can hear you."

His eyes go wide and he gets up from the couch that he's been perched on since he got home from work. "You're absolutely certifiable right now...do you know that? I can't wait until you have this baby so that your hormones go back to normal. Crazy Lav was fun for a while but Christ. You can't even stick to one rant at a time anymore."

So, I may have also become a bit more confrontational than I've ever been lately. I really don't know what it is but even if Rocco breathes too loudly it annoys me.

I'm not even going to get into the fact that his stupid chiseled jaw clicks every single time that he eats something. It's in between a grinding and clicking sound and drives me absolutely batty. I never realized that you could love someone so much but want to get rid of them at the same time.

And oh my gosh, he acts like I'm torturing him by asking him to put away his laundry. I even do the laundry for him. All he has to do is just either hang it up or fold it...that's all. Does he do that? Nope! He lays it flat all out all over our bedroom for days before he decides to put any of it away. At that point it's time to do another load again!

I love him, I truly do. He really is an amazing partner to have. But I swear, I might kill him before our son decides to grace us with his presence. I really don't know how much more of his heavy breathing while I'm trying to sleep that I can take.

"I am not certifiable. I'm upset that you've known for a week about tonight and couldn't be bothered to tell me about it so that I would have ample time to get myself ready." I huff. Not only are my arms crossed but now my foot is tapping.

He grabs onto his short hair and tugs while he starts pacing around the living room. "You act like I purposely didn't tell you just so that you would have to go looking like a homeless person."

"Ah ha!" I screech like a demented psychopath. "I knew it! You do think that I look homeless in this outfit." I say triumphantly.

He's now stopped in his tracks and is standing in front of me with his mouth hanging open. "Do you hear yourself right now Lav? You were the one who said you looked homeless, I was just repeating what you said. Baby, you need to take the crazy level down a few hundred notches."

He walks up and grabs my cheeks between his hands. "I love you but you're insane. Like the type of crazy that other crazy people are afraid of. Like padded room type shit these days babe."

I face plant into his chest and wrap my arms around his trim waist. "I'm not that bad." I mumble out my lie.

I can feel his body shaking. "Honey if you were any worse, your head would start spinning around." He places a kiss to the top of my head. "Now come on, I'll help you get ready, so that we won't be too late."

"Fine." I sigh.

I'm doing much better a few hours later after having eaten and had dessert. Unlimited chips and salsa can really brighten a pregnant woman's day. We're all eating at the Mexican place in town. I would think that they would want to stay far away from here after what happened to Marc, but everyone likes the food too much.

"I can't believe that you two are still pregnant." Mellie says merrily. I'd be happy too if I'd downed three margaritas.

"None of us can." Kay mumbles around her straw. "At least you don't have to deal with them too much like some of us do."

"What's that supposed to mean?" Sage growls like a junkyard dog.

"That you're two of the most miserable bitches that I've had the displeasure of being near." Kay says without missing a beat.

"We really haven't been that bad." I try to defend even though I know that it's total bull crap.

Everyone at the table just stops and stares. Sage and I look at each other, her with pursed lips, while mine are thin. It's not like we've killed anyone...geez.

"I'm old, I'm pregnant, I was so close to being free to just enjoy my life without having to worry about a kid. So excuse the fuck out of me if I'm a little bit unhappy while pregnant. Besides being old, I'm also as big as a house and have heartburn bad enough to burn down a village." My sister says ever so eloquently.

"Well then you should've listened to your kids and used condoms." Kay says while everyone else seems too afraid to even breath.

Everyone looks at me and I just shrug. "She pretty much covered the bases."

"Right." Declan claps his hands with a smile that's just a little too bright. "So, how about we talk about something else. Anyone throw anyone else's ex in front of a car lately?"

Sage, Kay, JJ, Rocco and I all turn in unison to look at Marc. Mellie looks at us and narrows her eyes at her brother. "Bubs, what the hell did you do now?"

"Nothing." He says before shoveling a huge amount of burrito into his mouth.

"Anyone dead or in the hospital?" Michelle asks him and he shakes his head no. She looks over to Mellie. "See, there's nothing wrong."

"Hey Shell?" Declan asks with an odd look on his face.

She gives him a bright smile. "Yeah."

Declan looks like he's choosing his words carefully. "Do you ever think that you maybe shouldn't have married my brother?"

A frown comes over her face, while Damon starts glaring at his twin. "No, why?"

Declan shakes his head slowly. "No reason." He gives her a small smile. "No reason at all."

"What happened?" Morris asks looking resigned to the fact that he might have to help them at some point. He's not looking forward to it judging by how he's currently chugging his beer.

Marc swallows his food and takes a sip of his beer. "The weirdest thing happened not too long ago. Lavender's ex actually almost hit me with his car."

"I'll bite." Damon says while leaning back in his chair. "How'd you end up almost getting run over by her ex?"

Marc gives him a creepy blank look. "I accidentally walked out into the middle of the street when he was driving by Sage and JJ's house."

"So, you threw yourself in front of his car." Declan casually states. "Did it occur to you that he might not stop?"

"No, because it's a natural reaction to jam on your brakes when you see something pop out in front of you." Marc plainly states like it's completely normal that he wasn't even the least bit worried.

Declan's eyebrows go up and then down. "Right." He grabs a chip and tosses it into his mouth. "What happened after that?" He asks while chewing loudly.

Gah...why is that so irritating?

"He got out of his car and we all had a nice little chat." The smile that crosses Marc's face gives me goosebumps and not the good kind that Rocco's touch gives me.

"He got out of his car and had a chat?" Damon asks while tilting his head to the side like a boxer dog does. Except he looks big and menacing and not cute like the puppies.

Marc nods his head. "More or less."

I look up at Rocco and poke him in his side to get his attention. "You never did say what exactly happened all that time you guys were in the garage that day."

Rocco looks down at me and gives me his charming little boy smile that means he full of crap. "We just had a nice little chat like Marc said."

"You know damn well that no one at this table is buying that load of bullshit. You guys wouldn't know how to be good even if there was a manual. Face it, you guys just attract trouble and always seem to welcome it." Mellie drawls, but she's not wrong.

"I'm hurt that you think that. I can't believe my own sister thinks that I purposely get into trouble." Marc pretends that a knife is sticking out of his heart.

"Cut the crap. Everyone knows that you were most likely the ring leader too. You just can't seem to help yourself, no matter what." She shakes her head at him.

"I happen to think that I'm an excellent friend for going above and beyond all the time for everyone."

"Don't act like you don't enjoy it." Kayla huffs. "You live for making trouble."

"As my wife, you should be supportive of whatever brings me joy." He sniffs.

"You ran out in front of a car. Do you really not see why I'm not patting you on the back?"

"You can skip the back pat if you'd like to pat other areas instead." He replies casually with a wicked gleam in his eyes aimed directly at his wife.

"Oh my God! I'm freaking eating! Stop...just stop!" Mellie gags.

Declan claps his hands again. "Back to the primary topic. Seriously, this group is like a bunch of kids with ADD when it comes to staying on topic."

I purse my lips and look up at the man studiously ignoring the fact that he knows darn well that I'm staring at him. "Yes, back to that little chat that you all had in the garage."

Rocco, JJ and Marc couldn't look anymore guilty if they tried. Rocco is looking anywhere but at me, JJ is keeping his head down and seems overly interested in his refried beans and rice. And Marc...well, he actually seems to be enjoying this. Geez these guys are so strange.

Marc rolls his eyes at his two cohorts that are obviously not going to be any help. "It wasn't that big of a deal really. We asked him why he was driving by. He gave a bullshit answer about wanting to check up on Lav after seeing her earlier that day." I can't even help the snort that comes out of me.

"And then Danny reminded him of what he told him what would happen if he ever came near Lav, Sage and Kay ever again. No biggie." He shrugs.

Kay, Sage and I look at each other and then at Marc. Sage decides to be the one to broach this particular topic. "And what exactly did Danny say would happen if he ever came near any of us?"

I mean, I'm sure that we all have a pretty good idea considering that it's Danny and all. He's a lot of things and protective is at the very top of the list. He was like the annoying big brother that I never wanted, especially when I was a teenager. So, yeah, I'm almost positive about what he told him.

Marc gets the creepiest smile on his face that I have ever seen in my entire life. "He told him that he would kick the shit out of him if he ever came near you girls again." He says with no small amount of glee.

I look around the table and sigh. "Fine, I'll ask. What happened at the end of this chat before Derrick went home?" I can feel the muscle above my eye twitching and my stomach is feeling queasy. I just know that Derrick didn't leave in the same state that he arrived.

"Why Lavender, sweet, sweet Lavender. You've known Danny for a long time. You should know by now that he's a man of his word." Marc says grinning like a loon. The two fools that were with him chuckle darkly.

I give the dope that I live with the stink eye that he pretends not to see. "And let me guess, the three of you didn't try to stop him at all?"

Rocco looks down at me with an innocent look that is completely out of place on his rugged face. "I mean honey, he was warned. He needed to learn that you can't just go around ignoring what other people tell you." He says solemnly.

"There is something so wrong with all of you guys." Kay states while shaking her head.

Marc looks down at her with a raised eyebrow. "Don't act like you won't be pressing me for details later on Pixie. You aren't exactly a huge fan of his."

She narrows her eyes and pokes him in the chest. "Yes, but at least I hide my blood thirstiness. Unlike you guys who let it all hang out for the whole world to see. Will I be crying that he got his ass handed to him? Obviously not, he's a huge douche canoe. But you guys are police officers for Christ's sakes. Try and act the damn part every now and then."

"I feel like the women in this group were a lot nicer before they married you guys. Even Lav has turned into a snarky bitch these days." Declan says while shaking his head sadly.

"Hey!" I yell. "I am not even close to being that bad!" I grunt and cross my arms over my ever-expanding chest. Of course, my man seems to have a specific radar for when my breasts are being pushed up and is now staring down at them with a glazed over look. I elbow him in the side. "Knock it off." I snap my fingers by my face. "Eyes up here buddy or you won't be seeing them for a long time."

Declan nods his head. "You're right. You're as sweet as pie." He says condescendingly, getting a chuckle out of everyone.

I glare at one of my closest friends. "Watch it Loki. No one really needs a two for one deal."

Damon actually spits out the sip of beer that he was taking and starts coughing. Shell pats him on the back while giggling. Sage and Kay pretend to wipe tears from theirs eyes. "I'm so very proud of you. You're finally the little sister that I always knew that you could be." Sage tells me while she rubs my hair like a psychopath.

"I'll remember this Lav." Declan sniffs and eats a chip.

Mellie snorts loudly. "So will the rest of us. It was a beautiful thing to hear." She starts laughing and everyone else joins in, much to Declan's chagrin.

"Anyway, forgetting about my sister's new-found awesomeness. How bad of shape was Derrick in when he left our house that day?" Sage looks at her husband who gives her a sweet smile.

JJ just gives her a little shrug. "Eh, I mean he walked out of the garage." Unfortunately for him, Marc and Rocco snort at the comment, causing my sister to give her husband a questioning look.

JJ glares at his two accomplices and then gives Sage a sheepish smile. "Walked...limped. It's the same difference really. All that matters is that Danny got his point across and I'm sure that we won't be seeing Derrick around for a long time."

Rocco groans from my side and places his head in his hand. "Now why the hell would you go and say that?"

"What do you mean? What did I say?" JJ asks with confusion marring his face.

Marc just shakes his head at him. "You know damn well that you should never say something like that. Because you did, we're now going to see that sack of shit everywhere."

Morris, Damon and Declan all nod their heads in agreement, while JJ moans. He holds up his hands. "I forgot! It was just a slip of the tongue. It doesn't mean anything."

"Aren't you guys being a little superstitious?" Mellie asks while sucking down another margarita. How many has she had already?

Declan shakes his head profusely. "Nope, it's the rule of the galaxy. Just like in horror movies how the virgin will only live as long as she doesn't go up the stairs instead of out the front door. You never," he gives JJ a nasty look, "ever say some stupid shit like JJ just did. We're all screwed now and not in a good way."

I hold up my hand. "Wait, I don't understand. How are all of us screwed?"

They all stare at me with wide eyes. I just huff. "That one isn't too bad of a word okay?" I mumble.

I can feel Rocco shaking next to me while Sage unwelcomely rubs my hair again. "I'm so proud of you. It's like you're all grown up now."

I turn my head and glare at her. "I hope that you don't lose any of your baby weight."

She gasps loudly and shoves my shoulder. "Take that back right now."

"Stop being annoying." I counter.

"So, why are we all screwed?" Shell asks ignoring my sister and I.

Declan looks at us and then to her. "Because, we were all sitting here together when he said it. Therefore, it now applies to all of us. He just jinxed us all."

"It doesn't count because I didn't really mean to say it." JJ grumbles.

"Oh yeah?" Marc drawls with his eyebrows raised. "Then explain this shit to me." He points towards the front door and I actually have to do a double take.

"Oh my gosh, you have got to be kidding me." I gasp.

Mellie looks towards the door and then back at me while clucking her teeth. "That's your ex isn't it?"

I nod my head. "Yup."

She looks over at JJ. "Good job big guy. Anything else you want to curse us with today?"

JJ palms his head. "It's not like I meant for this dammit." He groans.

"Yeah, but we're all going to have to pay the price anyway." Morris chimes in.

"It's a busy road out front." Damon supplies and we all just stop and stare at him. He gives us all a glare. "I'm just keeping all of our options open, that's all." He shrugs. "Ungrateful bunch of assholes." He mutters.

Sage looks around at all the men. "Seriously though, do any of you take the fact that you're police officers to heart?"

"Of course we do sweetheart." JJ looks at the rest of the men with wide eyes. "Right guys?"

He gets a round of grunted "yeahs". Good grief these men.

He looks back at my sister who's giving him a dirty look with a pleasant smile. "See, we all take our job very seriously."

"Right. That's why this one," Sage tilts her head in Damon's direction, "is offering to push someone out into traffic."

Marc scratches his face thoughtfully. "In his defense, he's pretty good at it."

Damon shakes his head. "Don't help me."

"That makes it so much better." Sage says sarcastically.

The guys just shrug, looking like they don't have a care in the world. They would definitely pull this look off, if all of them weren't clenching and unclenching their fists, while glaring daggers at Derrick. Honestly, my sister is right. These guys are a huge bunch of alphaholes.

"Can we just finish up dinner without someone getting injured, please?" I ask and bat my eyelashes at Rocco.

He smiles down at me. "Absolutely sweetheart." He says and then mumbles. "As long as he doesn't start any shit."

My lips thin. "Rocco." I hiss.

"What?"

"You know exactly what. Can't you just be good for two minutes?" I ask.

He gives me his panty melting smirk, oh boy. He nuzzles his face against the side of my neck. "You never have any issues when I'm being bad at home. I seem to recall that you like it a lot when I'm bad."

I can hear the guys cough out a laugh, while the women giggle quietly. I can feel that my face is the same color as a fire hydrant. I shove him away with all my might, not even moving him a centimeter. "Keep it up and the next time that you're bad, you and the couch can become best friends again."

"Oh, burn!" Declan says gleefully.

Shell looks at him with a frown. "Do people even still say that anymore? I thought that went out like years ago?"

"I haven't heard any of the girls say it. But they say a lot of weird and random shit that makes no sense." JJ tells us.

"Like what?" Mellie as with a new margarita in her possession. Seriously, when is she ordering those things? I haven't seen our waitress in forever.

"They say things like, *"that was lit"*, and other shit."

We spent the rest of dinner talking about all of the slang that none of us understand these days. While most of it was hysterical, I just couldn't shake the feeling that something bad was going to happen. Even now on the drive home, I still have that gut feeling. Okay, or it could just be indigestion from the six – don't judge me, I'm eating for two – tacos that I ate at dinner.

"You okay honey? You've been quiet since we got into the truck." Rocco asks me as well pull onto our street.

"Yeah, my stomach is just all wonky."

I look over at the sound of his snort. "I told you those last two tacos were a bad idea." He chuckles. "I'll get you the bottle of Tums and some ginger ale when we get inside."

When he isn't being the most annoying human being with his chewing and breathing, I really love him. "Thank you."

He quirks his lips. "Don't mention it."

He pulls into the driveway and I wait until he comes around to my side. It really is one of my most favorite things about him. I love that he's so sweet and caring.

We walk into the house and Rocco goes to get me stuff to settle my stomach. I walk down the hall and stand in the doorway of the nursey. I rub my tummy when I feel the little – well not so little – guy kicking around. He feels like he's trying out for the Olympics or something tonight.

I lean against the wall and just stare at the room that's lit up by a night light. We painted it a seafoam green and covered it with everything puppies that we could find. Rocco and I both want to get a dog but decided that it would be best to wait until after the baby was born so that they could grow up together.

I look over at the crib and can't believe that soon our little man will be sleeping in there instead of in my belly. As much as pregnancy really isn't any fun, I am definitely going to miss feeling him at all hours of the day. There really is no way to accurately describe what it feels like to have a piece of you moving around inside of you.

I rub my stomach again and have to bend forward after a particularly large kick. If this kid doesn't become a soccer player, it's going to be a darn shame.

Rocco seeing me hunched over practically runs up to me. "What's wrong sweetheart? Is it the baby? Are you guys okay?" He asks in rapid succession.

I giggle at how worried he gets over everything. The first time the baby kicked, I thought that he was going to have a full-blown panic attack. "I'm fine babe. This little one is just kicking away."

"Maybe it's his way of telling you that those last two tacos, plus my refried beans and rice, were a bad idea."

"I was hungry." I defend. Plus, come on, who doesn't over eat at a Mexican restaurant.

Name one person that you've ever met who doesn't walk out of there like a stuffed pig. If they don't, get far away from that person. They're probably a serial killer or worse a hippie vegan. Hmm, Kay's hatred for Max's teacher is getting bad these days. Although, in all honestly, she really is super annoying. It stinks having to work with her.

"I know honey, I know." He says condescendingly. "Let's go on in to bed babe. Maybe laying down with a pillow propped up behind you will help."

I give in because going to bed sounds like a great idea. Although, I have no interest in sleeping or just laying propped up. Thanks to my crazy hormones, I can't seem to get enough of Rocco.

And come on, him naked is a thing of pure masculine beauty. It really isn't too much of a hardship that my hormones make me crave him twenty-four-seven. He hasn't seemed to mind in the slightest either. If anything, he's the one who is always ready to go to bed, even if it's only seven o'clock at night.

Granted, I've been so tired lately that I've been passing out at like eight. But still, he has been overly excited about bedtime these past couple of months.

We walk into our bedroom and I take the Tums and wash it down with the ginger ale, before going through my nightly routine. While I wash my face, brush my teeth and change into pajamas, Rocco goes around the house checking for...well I have no idea. He calls it locking up, which I don't get since we lock the doors. I don't know what else he locks up, but whatever, if it makes him happy, so be it.

Once we're both in bed and laying under the covers, I snuggle – as best as I can with a beach ball in front of me – up to him. I place my head on his chest and look up into his amazing hazel eyes. "Hey Roc?"

"Yeah babe, what's up?"

"Will you give me a back massage?" I bat my eyelashes at him for good measure.

He purses his lips and gives me a questioning look. "Do you actually want a back massage or is this a code for sex? I just want to make sure because the last time you said this, I thought you wanted sex when you really wanted a massage."

I roll my eyes. "That was one time."

"I know but you completely freaked out and started crying that the only thing that I ever think about is sex. I just want to make sure that I'm not about to step on a landmine or anything here."

I prop my head up with my arm. "You are totally taking the sexy out of sexy time...do you know that?" I grumble. I mean...for real.

If looks could kill...well, I still wouldn't be dead. But she does look like a pissed off kitten who's about to scratch my eyes out. But damn, I'm just making sure that we're on the same page. I do not want a repeat of the last time.

She looked like she was about to cut me when I thought it was sex that she wanted. How the hell was I supposed to know? She asked all seductively and shit. Damn, you can't blame a man for going directly to that thought.

Then she spent the rest of the night either crying or glaring at me for being so uncaring and only thinking with my junk, her words. So, yeah, I'm going to double check so that I don't have a replay of that nightmare...sue me.

"I'm just making sure sweetheart." I croon. I definitely don't want to piss her off if it's sex she wants.

She gives me a pout. "You totally took the sexy out of it."

Oh hell no. This kid will be here any day, which means we won't be having sex for a while. Thanks to my brother-in-laws' bitching, I unfortunately know all about the time frame. We are getting in as much sex as possible now.

I jump out of bed and rip my t-shirt off. I also make sure to flex my abs for good measure. She seems to enjoy staring at them all the time. What my love wants, she gets. If it happens to benefit me in some way...so be it.

And just like I was hoping for, her eyes start to get that glazed look and she licks her lips. Thank God for her crazy ass hormones. The only time they aren't a pain in the ass, is when we're in bed. In bed, I fully support them being out of whack.

I drop my sleep pants and boxers at the same time. I just stand here in front of her for a minute. She's told me on several occasions how much she always enjoys the view. She takes a moment to look before she rips her nightgown over her head.

I raise my eyebrows. "No panties?"

She gives me an adorably sheepish look. "I decided not to bother since they would be coming off anyway."

"Have I ever mentioned how much I love the way you think?" I ask as I prowl towards her.

"Once or twice." She murmurs as she watches my approach. I can see how dilated her pupils are already and I haven't even touched her yet.

I crawl into bed again and lean over her. Thanks to her belly getting bigger, we've had to figure out some creative ways to have sex. It's been fun but I miss being able to stare deep into her eyes while I'm inside of her. I'm definitely looking forward to that once little man is born.

She has herself propped up on her elbows watching me get closer and closer to her. I run my nose along her cheek and inhale. She always smells sweet, like the best dessert in the world, times ten. With dessert in mind, I lick my way down to her collar bone.

She is completely pliant in my arms. It's a far cry from the nervous woman months and months ago. The more secure she becomes with our relationship, the more she seems to just let go and enjoy herself. Her embracing this part of herself is the sexiest thing that I have ever seen.

I still enjoy the blush that comes over her face anytime I bring it up. Some things will hopefully never change, that blush being one of them.

"Rocco." She mumbles.

"Yeah honey?" I ask while licking and sucking at all the sensitive spots around her neck.

"As much as I love how much you like to take your time, I've been ready to go since you put your hand on my thigh at dinner."

I lean backwards and look her in the eyes. "Babe, there was nothing sexual about that. I was literally just resting my hand there."

She starts biting on her full bottom lip again and shrugs. "I can't help it. It's not my fault that my hormones are crazy and get excited whenever you touch me."

I blink at her a few times. "Anytime that I touch you?"

"I mean, not when we're in front of your parents or anything, thank goodness. But yeah, I can't always help what my reaction is going to be."

"How long has this been going on?"

She takes a moment to think. "The last four months maybe."

My eyes widen and I gape at her. "You mean to tell me that we could've been having sex at any moment of the day. Anytime and anywhere? Like we could've had sex that time you asked for my help in that dressing room? We could've had dressing room sex and you never told me?" I ask incredulously. Months of kinky sex wasted!

"Are you kidding me right now? You're upset because we didn't have sex in a gross dressing room? Who in their right mind would want to have sex in a place like that?" She huffs.

"I would!" I ignore the disgusted look that she gives me and continue on. "I'm a man. We like to have kinky, random ass sex with the woman we love. The dirtier the better. Months babe," I gently grab her cheeks to implore her to understand what I'm saying, "months we could've been having freaky sex at a moment's notice. All of that time...just gone."

"Rocco honey." She says in a saccharine voice. "If you don't get over the fact that you missed out on sex in places that would most likely cause us to contract a disease, I can guarantee that you will be missing out on a lot of boring sex as well." She gives me a creepy smile that says I'm on thin ice.

I chuckle and try to back pedal as quickly as I can. "I was just kidding honey. Of course, I wouldn't want to just have sex in a random dressing room." I manage to keep the whimper out of my voice...barely.

"Uh-huh." The look that she's giving me says that she doesn't believe my lie in the slightest. "Can we maybe talk later? Otherwise, I'm going to find my battery-operated friend who is never disappointed about what goes on."

Fun fact that I've learned these past few months. Horny Lavender is blunt as hell and has no shame at all. It's interesting to watch her go from morally sound, to talking about a vibrator that will never be coming near her again.

"The fuck you will!" I growl before covering as much of her body as I can. I look into her eyes so that she knows how important what I say next is. "I am going to make sure that anything battery-operated is in the trash before you even realize it's missing. And why do you even have them...you have me?" I ask only slightly offended.

She rolls her eyes at me like I'm a moron. "I was single for years before we met Rocco." She sighs.

"Right." I mumble. "Yeah, that makes sense."

She snorts like a tiny piglet. "Ya think?"

I cough into my hand. "So, where were we?"

"Hopefully we're finally going to get to the good part." She mutters grouchily. Okay, point taken.

I slide my hands up her arms and towards her neck. I start massaging over her shoulders and neck in a hope to get her back in the mood. I don't know what it is, but a quick massage seems to do the trick every time.

I dig a little deeper into her neck and get rewarded with a sexy as hell moan that she doesn't even mean to be sexy. That's one of the things that I love most, the fact that she is so effortlessly sexy and doesn't even try. She's every wet dream that has become my reality. My only wish is that I met her sooner and could've had even longer loving her.

When she's nice and relaxed again, I start nibbling my way down her ear and neck. I hit the sweet spot right where her neck and shoulder meet. She grabs onto my hair to try to keep me in place. Sorry sweetheart, not right now.

I'm hoping that my self-control lasts long enough for me to make sure she's extremely happy. My dick has been harder than granite, even through our conversation. All I have to do is look at her and I'm hard. I feel like a damn teenager with his first crush all over again. She even makes my palms sweaty when she smiles at me to this day.

I lower my head and take one rosy nipple into my mouth while massaging the other with my hand. She tastes like cinnamon, sugar and mine...all mine. I make sure to lavish attention onto her other breast, making her moan and rub her legs together.

"Rocco please, no more teasing, I need you now. I have been ready for hours." She whines.

I smile inwardly, such an impatient girl. "And just think about how amazing it will feel when I finally decide to move lower."

I chuckle darkly at the little growl she gives me. She's actually trying to pull my head up, while wrapping – trying and failing – her legs around my waist.

"No more, I need you inside of me now." She says while still trying to get me to do her bidding.

"But sweetheart, I purposely skipped dessert because I knew that you would be mine when we got home." I give her a smirk that she glares at.

"You don't need dessert. Dessert is totally overrated and not good for you."

"Yeah, but it will be good for you." I say before parting her legs. She gives a half-assed attempt at closing them, but we both know that she really wants me to continue.

The first swipe of my tongue on her core has her hips shooting off the bed. The only thing keeping her in place is my arm that's draped across her abdomen. I lick and suck everywhere except near that one little spot that she needs. She's white-knuckling the bed covers and is groaning loudly.

I feel another tug at my hair. I raise my eyes to hers, but make sure that I don't stop what I'm doing. I quirk an eyebrow. "I swear Rocco, if you don't do something soon, I am not going to be responsible for how you end up maimed or dead." She growls, her voice thick with need.

"All you had to do was ask honey." I say against her core making her eyes rolls back. Apparently, pregnant women are super sensitive, it was fun figuring out how much over the last several months.

I go back to my ministrations but make sure to include her clit. She starts mumbling incoherently, but I make out *"more"* and *"don't stop"*, every so often.

I add one and then two fingers into her core. I can never get over how tight she always is. My fingers actually have a tough time moving in and out of her. I scissor them to stretch her a bit, which generally makes her fly ever higher, and it's definitely doing that tonight.

She is gyrating her hips so forcibly that I'm actually struggling to hold her down. I speed up my fingers and my tongue. She's moaning loudly and starts gasping for breath. I can feel how close she is with how she's quivering around me.

Knowing that she needs just a little something to push her over the edge, I suck her clit into my mouth and gently bite down. Not enough to truly hurt her but just enough to give her the barest hint of pain.

And it worked like a charm. Her entire body seizes up and goes stiff as a board. Her mouth is open as if she's screaming but nothing is coming out. I continue moving my fingers to draw out her orgasm as long as I can for her.

After a minute she goes boneless, with a goofy grin on her face. Her face is flushed, eyes glazed and hair rumpled. It's the best look that I've ever seen on her.

I slowly kiss my way up her body, giving her a few more seconds to recover. I would try for longer but my dick isn't having any of that right now.

She gives me a quick peck on the lips before she rolls onto her right side. I slide up behind her and run my hand over her stomach. This is one of the only ways we really can make it work with her being so far along in her pregnancy.

I nuzzle the back of her neck and lift her left leg, so that it goes over my hip. I kiss her shoulder and neck a few times before slowly sliding inside of her. I swear it gets better and better every time I'm inside of her. Her body feels like it was made just for me. If I could, I would spend the rest of eternity right here.

I always have to give her a few minutes to get accustomed to my girth no matter what. When she starts wiggling her hips, I begin to pump in and out of her. I start off slowly to get into a rhythm but that doesn't last very long.

My dick seems to have a mind of his own tonight. He thinks that we should be barreling in and out of her tonight like our life depends on it. I raise myself up a bit on my right arm to get better leverage and keep my left massaging each breast.

My pace gets faster and faster. The pace that I've set is brutal and her whole body is bouncing around. "You okay babe?" I ask sounding like a two pack a day smoker.

"Harder." She says breathlessly.

Okay then, I guess I'm not hurting her. With her encouragement I pound into her harder and harder. I can feel that all too familiar tingle at the base of my spine but I can't go without her getting off again. I absolutely refuse to be that guy who leaves his woman hanging.

I lower the hand that was playing with her nipples, down to her core. With the way each of us are slapping against each other, it's actually hard to get a grip on her. I finally manage to find her clit and start to rub circles around it furiously. I know that I'm not going to last much longer.

"Come on honey, come for me." I grunt out in an inhuman voice that signifies how close to the edge I am.

After a few more seconds, I finally feel the first telltale signs of her orgasm. When it hits, it shocks me with the force that her channel grips my dick. Not able to hold off any longer, I come with a long groan. Her body is literally milking me for every last drop.

When I can finally slide my dick out of her, I do so with an oddly loud pop. I roll onto to my back and try to catch my breath. She's laying next to me sounding like she just ran a marathon. Damn...we probably need to start working out more. We should not sound this bad after one round of sex.

She rolls her head over to look at me. "Have I ever told you how much I love that my hormones made me decide to take a chance on us?"

I look at her with a small glare. "That's all you've got to say after those dope ass orgasms?"

She starts shaking her head at me. "No, just no Rocco. We are way too old to be saying stuff like that. I'm in my late twenties and you're in your thirties. Things like that are for teenagers and others up until the age of like twenty-four. Those days are long gone babe."

"I'm not old. Thirty is like the new twenty or some shit." I mumble.

"No, it's not. Just accept the fact that you're getting older and you'll be a lot happier."

I'm about to reply when I suddenly feel all the wetness surrounding us. Damn, the wet spot has never been this big after sex. I mean, there tends to be a lot of fluid but shit, this is gross. We're definitely going to have to wash these sheets and put new ones on before we go to sleep. I am not sleeping in this shit.

"Hey babe? Have you recently become a squirtter and we haven't noticed?" I ask only slightly joking. I guess we could've missed that in the heat of the moment. Maybe it's another one of those weird pregnancy things.

She looks at me with a frown. "What are you talking about?"

I use my hand to motion to all of the fluid currently soaking our bed. "This wet spot is bigger than usual."

She looks down and her eyes get as wide as saucers. "Oh my gosh." She looks up at me with a look that's half excitement and half fear. "Oh my gosh!"

I rub her arm. "It's okay honey. We can just throw the sheets in the wash, it's not a big deal. We'll just keep a towel under us from now on or something."

She blinks at me a few times like she isn't comprehending what I just said. I know that those were great orgasms but damn, she must be tired.

She shakes her head and glares at me. "That's not from us having sex Rocco!" She hisses at me. "My water just broke, you big dope! That must've been that popping sound I heard."

Now it's my turn to blink at her. "What do you mean your water broke? That can't happen yet! We have another week before your due date!" I screech in an unusually high-pitched voice.

The look she's giving me is part, *I'm going to kill you,* and part, *you can't be this stupid.* "Babies come whenever they want to honey." She says slowly.

"Well tell him it's too soon! We're not ready yet."

Okay, later on, I know that I'm going to look back at this conversation and be amazed at how well she kept her calm and how much strength it probably took her not to slap me.

She's pinching the bridge of her nose and I can make out the fact that she's counting to ten in a mumble. "Yeah, it doesn't really work that way. He's going to come now, no matter what. He's pretty much the one in charge here, not us."

I jump out of bed and start running around our room aimlessly. Fuck! What the hell was I supposed to do? I snap my fingers, yes, the hospital bag! I need to take that out to the car.

I run into the living room, grab my keys pick up the bag and rush out to my truck. I unlock the door and toss the bag in the back. I run back into the house and see Lav standing in the middle of our bedroom with a look of shock on her face.

I run up to her and run my hands around her body. "Are you okay? Are you in pain? Do you need something? Why are you just standing here?" I rush out like a lunatic.

She blinks a few times and opens and then closes her mouth. "You went outside completely naked."

I look down and see that she is indeed right. I am completely buck naked and it didn't even fucking register. "I should probably get some clothes on, huh?" I ask sheepishly.

She nods her head slowly with pursed lips. "That would probably be a good idea. I'm going to take a shower, get dressed and then we can go."

"Are you crazy? We have to get to the hospital now! The baby's coming and you want to take a shower? Have you lost your mind?" Again, I'm going to look back and realize how much of a saint she truly is.

She places her hands on my cheeks and rubs them gently. "Honey," She starts in a soft voice, the kind that you use when speaking to a child, "we have plenty of time. I'm barely even getting contractions yet. The best thing for me to do, is to clean up and move around as much as possible. That will help everything progress nicely."

"Okay."

She gives me a smile. "Good. Now, while I'm showering, why don't you put some clothes on. You can't keep walking around like that. Once you have your clothes on, call my doctor's office and tell them that I'm in labor. Then call our families and let them know as well. Do you think that you can handle all of that?"

"Yeah, yeah, I got this. Don't worry about a thing babe. I'm totally on top of all of this." I lie through my damn teeth. I can't remember what to do after get dressed but I don't need her thinking that I'm any dumber right now.

"Okay...if you're sure?" She asks with a look that screams unease.

I give her a bright smile and a kiss on the lips. "Yeah sweetheart. You go shower, while I take care of everything else."

"Okay, thanks babe." She says before turning around and walking into the bathroom. I stay in place with the stupid smile on my face until she closes the bathroom door.

Holy fuck! I think to myself. She's having the baby. I try to calm down but the excitement pulsing through my body is unexplainable. I'm about to be a dad! Okay, now all I need to do is get dressed and remember all the shit that she just told me to do! One call to my sister Kellie to help me and she gets things going. First calling the doctor's office then Sage.

Once the doctor finally called me back, he said that we can head on over to the hospital whenever Lavender was ready to. I really don't understand how no one else seems to grasp the fucking concept that she's in labor and needs to be in the hospital. How am I the only one thinking clearly?

After calling Sage and listening to her scream into my ear about how she's on her way - lucky us – we said our goodbyes. Now I'm just pacing back and forth across the living room because the mother of my soon to be born child thinks that she should take the world's longest shower!

What the hell she's doing in there, I'll never know. You would think that she would just want to rinse off quickly, throw some clothes on and get to the hospital as quickly as possible. But oh no, not Lavender. No, she's having a damn spa day or some shit in there tonight.

I don't know what's more important than getting in my truck and driving to the nice place with a ton of doctors and nurses, but it must be good. Why she needs to take over thirty minutes to shower is just absolutely insane. Doesn't she want to get to the place with all the drugs?

That was one of the first things all of my sisters asked for when they were in labor. How is Lav not sitting in my truck drooling over the thought of her getting the good drugs?

"Okay I'm ready." Lav walks out and I shit you not, her hair and makeup are done. "Why are you looking at me like that?"

"You're in labor and you decided that doing your hair and makeup were more important than getting to the hospital?"

She rolls her eyes like I'm the one who is insane. "Rocco, my contractions are only nine minutes apart. We still have plenty of time."

I can feel my eyes bulge. "You're having contractions? Why didn't you say so before? We need to get into the truck right now. What is wrong with you woman? Do you want to have this baby on a floor without drugs?"

"Have you been drinking?" She asks with her head tilted.

"Of course I haven't been drinking." I growl. "Why would you even ask me that?"

Her lips quirk a bit and she gives me a bright fake ass smile. "No reason."

I motion my hands towards the front door. "Can we please get going already?"

"Yes honey, we can go. Don't worry, we'll be there soon." I choose to ignore the condescending tone of her voice. Doesn't she understand how stressful this is for me?

We finally...finally make our way to my truck. Once I get her situated, I run around and hop into the driver's seat. I start the engine, reverse out of the driveway and peel down the street.

I also ignore the way that she's clucking her tongue while glaring at me. I wouldn't have to drive like this if her crazy ass didn't need to dress up like she was going out for a night on the town.

I'm so focused on getting us to the hospital, that I don't even notice the car pulling out of the side street. One minute we're driving and the next thing I know, we're getting T-boned by an SUV.

We spin around several times and I throw my arm out in front of Lavender to make sure that she's okay. Her scream is loud enough to pierce my eardrum and is accompanied by shattering glass. It's over in a matter of seconds but feels like it took an eternity.

The air bags deploy and I stop the one in front of Lav with my arm that's still outstretched. It feels like I just got hit with a hammer. Motherfucker, that's going to leave a bruise. It can match the one that I'm sure I'm going to have on my face from where mine hit me.

Once the truck comes to a complete stop, I look over at Lavender. She's as pale as a ghost and is shaking profusely. She seems to have a few cuts on her where she has some blood trickling out of her. But other than that, I don't see anything major.

"Baby, look at me. Are you okay sweetheart?" I say while rubbing the side of her face.

The look in her eyes guts me. She has tears streaming down her face faster than I can wipe them away. She takes a large gulp of air. "I'm okay, I think." She stutters, sounding completely out of it.

"Honey, look at me real quick." I grab her cheek so that I can look into her eyes.

I sigh in relief when her pupils look fine. The last thing we need is for her to be in labor and shock at the same time.

I undo my seatbelt and hers and pull her towards me. I kiss her all over her face. She hugs me tightly around my middle. We stay like that for a few minutes until I remember about the fuckwad that hit us.

I look down at her. "Baby, I need you to call nine one one and tell them about the accident. I need to get out and make sure that the idiot who hit us is okay. But I need you to make sure that you don't move too much. Tell them that you're in labor and will be needing an ambulance. Do you think that you can do that for me sweet girl?" I croon lowly. Keeping her mind occupied on a certain task will be the best thing for her right now.

She sniffles a few times, but quickly gets her shit together like the amazing woman that she is and nods her head." Yeah, I can do that. Don't worry, I'm sure that I'm fine."

I kiss the side of her head. "I'm sure you are, but it's best not to move too much right now. I want to make sure that you and little man are properly taken care of, okay?"

She gives me a tiny smile. "Okay babe. Go check on that idiot and make sure that they're not hurt."

"I will. I'll be back in a few minutes." I say before trying to open my door.

Thankfully the SUV hit us on my side and not Lavender's. I'm definitely going to be feeling this shit tomorrow. And my door is pretty much crushed and not opening. I growl while breaking the rest of the glass on the window and knocking it out of the truck.

I somehow manage to squeeze my ass out of the window and almost fall straight down. The hit knocked off the running boards that I was hoping to step on. "What the fuck else tonight?" I mutter to myself.

When I look back through the window I see Lavender staring oddly at me. "What's up babe?"

She blinks a few times and gives me a frown. She pulls on her door handle and it swings wide open. "You could've just used mine instead of crawling out of a window that's covered in broken glass."

I scratch the side of my head. "Yeah, that wasn't even a thought for some reason."

"Yeah, no, why would it be? It's not like it's the easier or safer route to go."

I just shrug and give her a smile. "I'm a guy babe. We don't pay attention to easier or safer." I give her a wink before walking away.

The Lexus SUV looks like it's pretty much totaled. People wonder why I like big trucks, it's for this exact reason. Sure, my truck is fucked and probably totaled too, but at least it doesn't look like an accordion like this one does.

As I get closer I see that the driver appears to be a male. He pushes his door open and stumbles out before falling to the ground with a groan. As I walk over something strikes me as familiar about that voice but my brain is somewhat scrambled right now. But still, I keep getting that annoying gut feeling.

When I get to the driver's side of the vehicle and get a good look at the man lying on the ground I internally curse JJ seven ways to Sunday. I knew it! I knew that motherfucker had jinxed us! None other than Derrick is laying on the ground with blood trickling down from his temple. Son of a bitch!

But that's not the only shit part. This idiot reeks of booze. And not like he tied one on last night and it's just making it's way out of his pores. Nope. He smells like he just bathed in a barrel of whiskey. It's actually making me kind of nauseous to be honest. Of all the stupid shit to do, this moron drives drunk as a skunk.

I swipe my hand down my face and take a few deep breaths to calm myself down. Right now I want to rip out his throat, but I know that I can't. This fool could've not only killed my future wife – unbeknownst to her – and my unborn child, but he could've killed any number of others. Deep breaths in and deep breaths out.

I come out of my little mantra by his moaning. Good. I hope the fucker broke a few bones. It would serve his dumbass right. Realizing that I need to be the bigger person and act like the law enforcement official that I am I move – slowly...I'm not Ghandi – over to the dipshit.

"You okay?" I drawl not really giving a shit but pretending that I do.

"I hurt everywhere." He whines like a little bitch. I wonder if I could get away with just kicking him in the ribs once...maybe twice. Who's really going to believe a drunk over the sober police officer after all?

"That tends to happen when you drive drunk and crash into another vehicle." I deadpan.

He looks up at me with blurry, bloodshot eyes. "I'm not drunk." He slurs.

I snort. "Yeah, you look and sound totally sober man. Listen, do you think anything is broken?"

He tries and fails miserably to roll onto his stomach. "I don't know." He snaps. "Everything fucking hurts thanks to you."

I raise my eyebrows. "Thanks to me?" I chuckle darkly. "You're the one driving drunk and ran into my truck. You pulled out of a side street without looking. This is all your fault."

"I'm not talking about the fucking cars. I'm talking about the fact that one of your *buddies*" – he spits out – "payed Lilly a visit today. He decided to inform her that I have a girlfriend on the side. Thanks to you and my ex whore, my wife now wants a divorce and I won't get a penny. Too bad I didn't fucking kill you both...."

He passes out before I can even say anything or ask him any questions. It's just as well really. If he continued talking, I might not be able to keep a lid on my temper. Especially with him calling Lavender a whore.

I keep going over my deep breaths mantra. I continue to stand here because the last thing I need is for this moron to vomit and choke on it. Granted, I don't really care about his life that much, but it would look really bad if a cop let someone die. Although, I could probably just say that I was checking on Lavender at the time.

I could literally kick him a few times, maybe even *"accidentally"* step on his fingers and break a few. No one would ever know and I highly doubt that he would even wake up.

I sigh and shake my head at myself. I have never hated anyone the way that I hate this jackass. He is literally a stain on humanity and just a crappy human being. But that still doesn't mean that I can harm him. No matter how much it makes my soul happy to think about.

I run my hand over my hair and tug. The girls are right. There is definitely something really wrong with the group of us. We really are most likely the world's worst police officers. Though, I'm pretty sure a lot of men would be contemplating what I am, if they were in my current position.

He could've killed all of us. I don't think that I'm the world's worst person for just wanting a small amount of retribution. It's not like I would kill him. Just sort of maim him a tiny bit. He would still be fully functional, just a little worse for the wear, if you will.

I must've been contemplating this horrible shit for a while because all of a sudden I hear sirens getting closer and closer to us. Damn, I guess that I probably should've acted while I had the chance. The last thing that I need is someone seeing me do anything to this idiot.

So like the bigger man that I am currently pretending to be, I back away from Derrick and stand in between our two vehicles. Then it hits me again, I'm about to be a father! Holy shit!

No one ever tells you how much contractions hurt! Period cramps my butt! This feels like my body is being ripped apart from the inside out. I grit my teeth through another one as I cling to Rocco's hand. We finally made it to the hospital twenty minutes ago, after the whole debacle.

They took me right in for different testing and I was found to be in good health except for a few minor cuts from the shattered glass. Oh, and the fact that my labor had progressed swiftly thanks to the accident. Apparently, things like that can speed up the process...who knew?

I still can't get over the fact that it was Derrick. I mean of all the people in the world to be driving drunk and to hit us, of course it would be the black cloud of my past. I swear, I am going to give JJ a piece of my mind the next time I see him. This was all his fault!

Okay, I probably won't once I'm no longer in excruciating pain and hating every man in the world, since they never have to go through anything like this. But still, it's a nice thought for my currently grumpy mood.

My mood went downhill when they put me on an uncomfortable back board during my ambulance ride. Because that's what every pregnant woman in labor wants, to be even more uncomfortable.

"You're doing great baby." Rocco croons at my side, causing my eyes to cross at him. I love him, but I might kill him for doing this to me.

And don't give me that crud about it takes two to tango. I'm the one about to push a watermelon out of a hole the size of a darn lemon. I'm allowed to blame him as much as I want. All he has to do is just stand there in perfect health. Stupid men.

"Honey, if you keep talking to me like that, instead of grabbing my hand on the next contraction, I might *"accidentally"* grab somewhere else. You know, somewhere that would ensure that this never happens to me again." I tell him sweetly.

He blinks down at me a few times with his mouth hanging open. A snort from the nurse seems to bring him out of his daze. "Anything you say sweetheart." He says while casually hiding his balls from my grasp...chicken.

The person that I've been dying to see the most walks in and I couldn't be any happier. "Hello, I'm Dr. Shapiro and I'm the anesthesiologist."

Once the only man that I wanted to see today leaves, I am a much happier girl. The amazing things that a needle in your spine can do. I can finally relax a bit now that I don't feel like I'm dying.

Rocco is sitting in a chair across the room giving me a small smirk. "Feeling better?"

I narrow my eyes at him. "Yup." I say while popping the P. "He's my newest favorite person ever."

"And just think. If you hadn't taken a year and a half to get ready, you would've gotten to meet him sooner."

I roll my eyes. "Rocco, they only do it after you're a certain amount dilated. They would not have done it when my water first broke honey."

He crosses his arms and leans back in the chair. "You don't know that for sure." He grumbles petulantly. I swear, men are nothing but big kids some days. Actually, my kids in class are better than he is some days.

I just give him a smile and rest my head back against my pillow. No use arguing with a stubborn man when he has a stick up his butt. I know that his truck is totaled but geez, he's been acting like someone took away his favorite toy. He's been talking about getting a new truck soon, so I don't see why he's so upset.

"So, what did Derrick say to you that has you in such a bad mood?" I sigh, it really has to be something to do with him.

His cheek twitches but other than that his face remains somewhat impassive. "What do you mean babe?"

I roll my head to left to fully look at him. "Rocco, don't even try that with me right now. I'm in labor and about to pop out a huge baby. It's in your best interest to answer any questions that I ask right now."

He clucks his teeth. "You know, this pregnancy has made you very grumpy."

My eyes turn to slits. "Don't try changing the subject. What did he say to you to make you so mad?"

He leans forward onto his elbows. "What? I can't just be mad at the fact that he fucking drove drunk and almost killed us?"

I purse my lips and cross my arms and rest them on my massive belly. "You were just fine until you went to talk to him."

"I didn't know that the driver of the vehicle that hit us was drunk at the time. I thought that it was just a dumb and inexperienced teenager." He counters.

"Rocco!" I growl, my patience almost non-existent at this point.

His heads drops. "Fine, he said a bunch of bullshit about it being our fault."

I frown. "How in the world is him driving drunk our fault?" He is seriously delusional.

Rocco chuckles. "I guess one of my *"buddies"* as he put it, paid his wife a visit today. Whoever it was told her that Derrick had been cheating on her. I guess she wants a divorce and he won't get money or something. I don't really understand all of it, what with him slurring and all."

Hmm, there's something missing. "What else? I know that's not the only thing that made you mad."

He casually shrugs. "It might've pissed me off that he called you his *ex whore.*"

And there it is. My sweet man is upset on my behalf. A cute as it is, it's really unnecessary. I start to giggle and get an evil look from my love.

"Why are you laughing at that?" He hisses causing me to laugh even harder.

I actually have tears in my eyes by the time I'm able to compose myself. I swipe under my eyes a few times before replying. "Because honey, we both know that I'm not. So, what does it matter what he says or thinks? He doesn't matter at all in our lives. Why get yourself so upset on such an exciting night for us? Our son is about to be born. Focus on that babe, not what some drunken jerk says."

I can see him physically deflate. "I guess you're right." He says. "It still would've been nice to get a few kicks in though." He mutters, but I must be mistaken.

"What was that honey?"

He looks up at me with his little boy smile. "Nothing babe, you're right. Let's just get into a great mood to meet our little guy soon."

I narrow my eyes but let it go. I know darn well that he said something about kicking.

Forty-Five Minutes Later:

"Congratulations! It's a girl!" The doctor says much to our utter confusion.

Rocco and I look at each other and then look at the doctor that was on call. You can see the confusion plainly written all over our faces.

Rocco coughs into his hand. "What do you mean, it's a girl? We're having a boy."

I just nod my head in agreement. The doctor who looks like she's barely out of medical school quirks her eyebrow at us. She holds up the screaming baby and sure enough, it's a girl. Rocco and I just stare at the tiny baby in her arms, covered in some weird whiteish goo.

Rocco looks down at me with panic written all over his handsome face. "We can't have a girl right now. We need a boy first so that he can scare away any boys who come near her. This is not part of the plan!" He says in an oddly high-pitched voice.

I couldn't help the snort that I let out if I tried. "What plan? We got pregnant after a drunken night in Vegas. You decided to just tell everyone that we were together and moved yourself in. We literally have never had any sort of a plan throughout our entire relationship."

He throws up his arms. "I had a plan dammit. We were going to have a boy. Then on Valentine's Day, he was going to be wearing a cute little shirt that says 'Mommy is my Valentine' or something like that. Then you would open the present from him, only to find out that it was an engagement ring from me. Then we were going to get married and have a bunch more kids. Except they would all be boys, except for our last one who would be a girl that would have three big brothers to protect her. There was definitely a plan and now that's all shot to hell!"

You could literally hear a pin drop. Even our daughter stopped crying during her father's outrageous rant. My eyes are blurry and rapidly filling up with tears. "You're going to propose on Valentine's Day?" I hiccup.

You can see the moment that he realizes everything that he just said. "Obviously not now since that plan has been shot to hell in a hand basket."

I glare at him. "What do you mean not now?"

"How can I, it's all ruined." He shrugs. I might just kill him yet.

The doctor being an obviously smart woman picks up on my anger while the nurses chuckle quietly on the other side of the room with our daughter. She coughs a few times and gets his attention. "Hey Dad, what Momma here is asking, is do you mean that you aren't going to propose anymore? That's why she also looks like she's about to stab you with the scissors that I used to cut the cord."

He rolls his eyes. "Of course, I'm still going to propose, but now I have to come up with a whole different idea. Do you have any idea how long I've been planning that one?" He asks in a very much so put out tone. He then does a double take at the doctor. "Hey, wasn't I supposed to cut the cord?"

She gives him a shrug. "You were taking too long with your freak out. I had to get the baby to the nurses to get checked out and cleaned up."

"Oh." He says like a dejected two-year-old. Good grief, men are absolutely worse than children are.

I pat his arm condescendingly. "It's okay honey, you can cut the cord on the next one. You know, since we'll be having four kids and all." I drawl.

He looks down at me with a sheepish grin on his face and scratches the side of his head. "Probably should've mentioned that part to you before huh?"

"About how many children you think that we're having?"

He nods. "Yeah."

My lips thin. "No, why would you need to do that? I'm just the one who would be carrying them around for months and the one who would have to go through labor again. But it's not a big deal."

"I feel like you're being a little sarcastic here."

I look incredulously at the dope that I'm very much in love with and plan to marry, as long as I don't kill him. "What makes you say that?"

"Is this a trick question or are you serious?"

"Good Lord sugar, you need to shut that mouth of yours." One of the nurses says. "Your woman looks like she's two seconds away for murdering you. And let me tell you, I wouldn't do much to try to stop her right now."

He looks around at the other women nodding their heads in agreement and promptly shuts his mouth. Good choice babe...good choice.

The minute that our little girl is placed in my arms is a feeling like no other. I can't even begin to describe the amount of love that I feel for this tiny baby that now depends on me. There is no greater feeling that having her in my arms, nestled up against me. This is one of those moments that I'll remember for the rest of my life.

I look up in time to see Rocco pointing his phone at me. "Beautiful, absolutely beautiful." He says with awe lacing his voice.

"You want to hold her?" I ask, even though I don't really want to give her up just yet.

He nods his head excitedly and I can't even be upset with how adorable he looks right now. I gently pass her over and watch as he cradles her like she's the most precious thing in the entire world. And I'm pretty sure that if there was any part of my heart that he didn't already own, he most certainly owns it now.

The look of pure love and rapture on his face is one of the most amazing things that I have ever gotten to witness. I can't even keep my sniffle in check. He looks so perfect holding her right now.

He looks at me in alarm. "Why are you crying?"

I giggle at his look of panic. "They're happy tears, I promise."

"If you say so." He says dubiously while raising our little girl to his face and inhaling. He looks back at me again. "What should we name her?"

And if that isn't a good question. We didn't pick out any girl names since we were told that we were having a boy. How that technician messed this one up, I'll never know.

He gets a wicked grin on his face and nothing but mischief swimming in his eyes. "Hey, you want to follow in your parents' footsteps and name her Vegas?"

I glare at him. "No." I hiss. "We are not doing what my parents did. We can come up with a proper name, thank you very much."

"You sure? It will definitely be a good ice breaker for her later on in life when people ask her about her name."

"Do you want to see her first birthday?"

He gives me a shrug. "Hey, I'm just trying to be helpful."

"Try a little less." I growl much to his amusement.

"Okay then, Miss Picky, what do you suggest?"

I choose to ignore his sarcasm, because I'm nice like that. "I guess we do need to stick with some sort of a tradition." I tilt my head and think. "Sage could probably be really helpful." It's just then that I remember that she was supposed to be here. "Where is she anyway? She promised that she wouldn't miss this."

Rocco passes me back our baby girl. "I don't know. Last time I talked to JJ after the accident, he said that they would be here. Let me give him a call."

I look down and coo at the precious little bundle in my arms. Rocco puts the phone on speaker so that I can hear. "Hello." JJ says out of breath.

"Hey man, where are you guys. We already had the baby."

JJ chuckles a bit on the other end. "Oh, we're at the hospital."

Rocco and I give each other a curious look. "Okay, then why don't you guys make your way up to Lavender's room?"

"Well, we would but Sage completely freaked out when she found out about you guys being in the accident. I guess the stress was a little too much because she literally just gave birth to Damian three minutes ago."

"No shit?" Rocco asks in shock and I'm right there with him.

"No shit." JJ says with pride lacing through.

"Damn, congratulations man. Would've thought that they would be conceived and born on the same night?"

"Rocco!" I screech and hear everyone laughing, including JJ.

"Congratulations to you guys too. How's your little man doing? Sage is dying to know."

"The technician was wrong." Rocco pouts.

"What do you mean?"

"We had a girl."

There's a long pause and then nothing but JJ cracking up. "Sage listen to this shit, they had a girl. The scan was wrong." He says laughing like a hyena. "Rocco had a bunch of shit planned out too. He kept saying how glad he was that he was going to have a boy first! Oh God, my side hurts. This has been the best night ever!"

"You know, you're still on speakerphone?" My grumpy man drawls.

"What's your point buddy?"

"You're an asshole." Rocco mumbles.

"Never said that I wasn't."

"Rocco, watch your language! How many times are we going to go over this! She'll pick up everything." I huff. Is it really too much to ask for him to clean up his language for our children?

"She's literally like ten minutes old. How is she going to pick that up? If she does, then we need to get her into MIT, Mensa or something, because that would be incredible."

I narrow my eyes while gently rocking our sleeping baby in my arms. "You know darn well that's not what I meant. Stop trying to change the subject because you're being bad again."

"Shouldn't your hormones be going back to normal already?" The dead man standing asks me.

"It takes six months for a woman's hormones to go back to normal after child birth."

His eyes bulge out of his head. "Are you kidding me? You're going to be crazy for another six months?"

"Sugar, sugar, sugar." The same nurse pipes in again. "Now is the time that you're going to be wanting to shut that trap of yours again. Nothing good is going to come from you continuing with this conversation." She shakes her head at him.

He looks around and then down at his phone and frowns. He looks up at me. "He hung up."

I snort. "Can you blame him?"

"I guess not. Still uncool though." He mumbles. He looks at me and wiggles his eyebrows making me laugh. "So, back to naming our little princess. What should we call her?"

Indeed, if that isn't the question of the day.

Epilogue

I can't believe that this day has finally arrived! I swear that it seemed to take an eternity to get here. But now that it's here, I don't want this day to ever end. I get to marry my very own Prince Charming today, in front of all of our friends and family.

And no, we did not go to Vegas, despite almost everyone trying to convince us to. Nope, we are getting married in the church that Rocco grew up in. Since my family isn't overly religious – unless my parents worshipping the earth count – I told Rocco that we would get married wherever he wanted.

That was actually the only time that his parents gave us any input and stately firmly that they would like for us to be married in the same church that they, including his sisters, were. I thought that it was a sweet tradition and readily agreed.

Now I'm standing in the back room putting the final touches on. My sister, who is my maid of honor, is here, along with my four other bridesmaids. I'll give you three guesses who they are!

I've been staring at myself in the mirror for the past five minutes. I can't believe the person staring back at me. To think that a few years ago I was unhappy and somewhat just going through the motions of life.

Then came Rocco barreling into my life like a wrecking ball, albeit a very handsome one, but a wrecking ball nonetheless. He completely turned my world upside down and I couldn't be anymore grateful for his stubborn nature.

To think that I could've missed out on every amazing moment that has happened since he came into my life, all because I was content to be a coward. I will be forever grateful that Rocco helped me find and nurture my backbone. Thanks to him, I'm still me, just a happier and more confident version of myself.

I run my hands down the length of my silk gown, marveling at the feel. I didn't choose pure white, since my daughter is the flower girl, it just seemed in bad taste. But when I saw this cream colored, silk mermaid gown, I knew it was the one. It even fit me like a glove, the moment that I tried it on. It was fate and came home with me that day.

It has Swarovski crystals around the stomach, acting as a sparkly belt of sorts. It's completely strapless, with a V cut front showing a modest amount of cleavage. It's tight until it gets past my knees and then goes out a bit.

I didn't want one of those big, poufy dresses. I know that some women go gaga over them, but I am definitely not one of them. Besides not really being able to get around easily in those things, I had no urge to need five people to help me pee. There are some things that other people should just not have to help you with.

I'm wearing my hair half up, with the bottom curled. The part that is up has a bun that my tiara is around. I also kept my makeup light as well. Since it's a nice spring day, I figured that light makeup would look the best. I just don't think that I could really pull off a smokey eye too well anyway.

"You look gorgeous." Sage sniffles as she stands behind me with her arms wrapped around me.

I smile at her in the mirror. "Thank you. You clean up pretty well yourself."

That's an understatement. All of my ladies look incredible in their dresses. I let them all pick out which style of dress they wanted, as long as it was the light blue that I wanted. Well, except for Sage, her dress is a shimmery sliver, spaghetti strap gown in silk, that looks amazing on her.

She stands next to me and appraises herself in the mirror. "Honestly, it's just nice not wearing something covered in baby vomit for once." She says with a smirk.

"Amen to that." I agree and hear murmurs of agreement from all the other ladies. Well, except Holly, since she's still single and kidless. I don't miss not having a child, but I really do miss sleep. She's so lucky getting to sleep.

Sage nudges me with her hip. "You ready for this? Cause if you're not just say the word. Dad said that he has a getaway car ready for you. Although, I'm sure that he's smoked again since he told me that and has probably forgotten already." She chuckles.

I look at her with wide eyes. "You let them bring weed...today? Are you kidding me? I thought that we agreed that they need to be on their best behavior today?"

She puts her hand on her hip. "Well, I was going to until I remembered what happened when we took their weed away during my wedding. Do you happen to remember that sister dear? How drunk they got because they're not used to drinking much. Do you remember how Mom and Dad were trying to get other couples to join them for "*some fun*"? Remember how mortifying it was having to give people bullshit excuses?"

I grimace because I remember exactly that. It was completely humiliating having them act like that. Sure, they're goofy when they're stoned but at least they don't act like horny teenage swingers. Good Lord, just remembering the look on JJ's parents' faces when my parents propositioned them. I don't think that they ever fully recovered from that.

Sage and I look over when we hear all of the girls cracking up. "Oh my God, I still can't believe that you two talk about your parents like this." Mellie giggles.

"In their defense, they really do need to be conscientious when it comes to their parents. I've been friends with Sage a long time and have seen things that you couldn't even dream up. Their parents really are something else. The sweetest people alive but they really don't like being conventional." Kayla laughs.

Michelle shakes her head while holding onto Damian. "I just can't get over that you two have to figure out how to take your parents' weed away. They sound like the teenagers and you two the parents."

Sage and I give each other a wary look. "In all honesty, it was kind of like that while we were growing up. They were the same as they are now. Sage and I barely had any rules at all. The only one that they really had was not to become some *"corporate schmuck"* as they like to say. Other than that, we were pretty much left to our own devices." I say while walking over to Mellie.

I look at my sweet little girl in her flower girl dress and Damian in his ring bearer tux and can't get over how adorable they look. They make the most adorable little duo in the entire world. Sure, I may be a bit biased, but they are the cutest babies in the universe.

And if you're wondering, yes we stuck with somewhat of a tradition. We ended up naming our sweet girl Violet Skye. I'm sure that she'll hate it when she's older but it is such a cute name. I could not be happier with our choice.

Motherhood has definitely been an interesting experience. Even with Rocco's mother watching Violet for us all the time, it is still exhausting. Little miss is a daddy's girl all the way though. So, I actually get more downtime than Rocco does.

The moment that he steps foot into the house, she demands his undivided attention. She knows that she has him wrapped around her little finger and uses it to her advantage. I can't even be upset that I have to wait until after she's in bed to get any time with my man.

They make the cutest pair when they're together. I can't even tell you how many pictures of the two of them that I have. But my favorites will always be with both of them asleep and Violet snuggled up on her daddy's chest. My heart gets so full every time that I look at the two of them.

I pick Violet up and blow raspberries on her neck making her giggle. There is no better sound in the world than a baby giggle. It's the purest sound and amazes me every single time that I hear it. Now being no different.

"You ready to help Momma get married pretty girl?" I coo at my soon-to-be-husband's mini-me. And isn't that some bull crap? I go through all the trouble of growing her and giving birth and she looks identical to him.

She makes her baby noises and tries to make a grab for my tiara. I bounce her up and down. "I'll take that as a yes."

Sage comes up and takes her from my arms. She gives Violet a loud, smacking kiss on her cheek. "No, no, sweet girl. Mommy has to look pretty and not disheveled right now. You need to keep those tiny little hands far away from Mommy right now."

We all turn towards the door when we hear the knock. "Come in." I yell.

My father pokes his head into the doorway and gives us a big smile. "I am being told that it's almost time and that everyone needs to get in their places."

Okay, I know that Sage and I joke relentlessly about our parents, but they really are the most amazing ones out there. They are nothing but loving and supportive. I really don't know what I would do without them and their unconditional love.

"Alright, we're out of here. I'll give you and Dad a few minutes." She says to me with a wink and then looks around. "I've got Violet, will someone grab the future demon please?"

I nudge her a bit. "You need to stop calling him that. He's been nothing but sweet."

"For now." She mutters. "Come on, chop, chop ladies." She says, sounding like Danny when he teaches a class.

Once everyone leaves the room, it's just my father and I. Now here's the thing about my parents. They don't look like typical hippies with long hair and weird clothing. My parents are always impeccably dressed and styled. My father is wearing a dark pin-stripe suit that I know was custom made.

What Sage and I never tell anyone, is that my father made a ton of money in the stock market before deciding that him and Mom should only have fun in life. No one would ever guess that my dad is a genius when it comes to money. Sage and I have decent accounts thanks to my dad's brilliance.

Dad walks up and wraps me up in his arms. He's actually a pretty tall and well-built guy, meaning he lifts me off the floor easily. He gives me a kiss on the cheek when he lowers me back to the floor.

"You look stunning my sweet little girl. Rocco is one of the luckiest men in the world."

I have to blink a few times to keep the tears at bay, stupid hormones are still not back to normal yet. "Thanks Daddy." I say lowly.

"You almost look as beautiful as your mother looked on our wedding day. Then again, no other woman will ever be able to compare to her in my eyes, even you and your sister." He says with that lovesick grin that he gets whenever he talks about Mom.

I don't even take offense to what he just said because I know that he truly means it. My mother is the most beautiful woman in the world to him and I love that. I love that they are both still so in love that they only see each other. Actually, wait a minute.

"Hey Dad?" I ask somewhat uncertainly.

He looks at me with a serene smile. "Yes baby girl?"

I'm not actually sure how to go about asking this. Even for our family, this one seems a little weird. But whatever, we're a weird family. "You remember Sage's wedding?"

"Yeah."

"You really love Mom right?" Geez, I really don't know how to go about this.

"More today than the day I said 'I Do.'" He states while giving me a curious look.

I start to fidget around a bit. This is just so awkward but I really want to know. I blow out a big breath and just decide to go for it. "If you love Mom so much and her you, why did you guys try to convince other people to, you know...join you guys."

Oh my gosh! My face feels like it's on fire right now! Seriously, why in the world did I decide that I needed to know the answer to this? I'm taken aback when my father bursts out laughing. And I don't mean like a little chuckle either. He is full on belly laughing. What could he find so funny about this?

It takes him far too long to get a hold of himself. He has tears streaming down his face and is holding his side when he finally looks at me again. "I was wondering when one of you were going to ask us about that. Truthfully, I really didn't expect it to be you though."

"You and me both." I drawl making him chuckle again. "But I just don't get it. You and Mom are so into each other that it just seems really weird."

He gives me a smile that I can't place. "And you would be correct. It would be very weird."

I frown and tilt my head. I put my hands on my hips and tap my foot. "But you did. I just can't believe that you guys would do that. And at Sage's wedding no less!" I huff.

"Oh, my sweet girls. You two really are too easy to screw with." He laughs.

I narrow my eyes. "What are you talking about?"

"Don't you think that we realize how uptight you both are when it comes to our lifestyle choice?" He quirks an eyebrow and continues. "Sometimes your mother and I like to have a little fun in life."

My nose scrunches up. "Eww Dad! That's disgusting! I change my mind, I don't want to know anymore."

He sighs loudly. "Not like that. I swear you and your sister are too easy. It was a joke Lav. Your mother and I decided that since you both took our *herbal supplements* away, that we would have a little fun at your expense." He starts belly laughing again.

"The looks on your faces when your mother started propositioning people was the funniest thing that I have ever seen. It took all of my might to keep a straight face. I really don't know how your mom pulled it off. I truly bow down to that glorious woman." He wipes at his eyes.

I blink at him a few times not fully able to comprehend what he just said. When I finally snap out of it, I realize that I'm going to need to find someone else to walk me down the aisle because I'm about to murder him.

"Are you kidding me? Do you have any idea how embarrassed we were? Everyone still laughs at us for that. It was absolutely humiliating!" I yell.

"Oh, I know that you two were embarrassed. You both turned bright red and started stuttering. Your mom and I still laugh about it whenever we're having a bad day. It never fails to cheer us right up." He says gleefully.

"I can't believe you both!" I hiss.

He crosses his arms and raises an eyebrow. "I guess you two shouldn't treat us like we're children then, should you?"

Darn. He may have a point but still. "It's for your own good. There's a bunch of police officers around. The last thing Sage and I need to do is bail you and Mom out of jail for drug charges."

He smirks down at me. "Uh-huh. I'm sure that's your motivation. You both definitely don't have any ulterior motives."

"Of course not!" I sniff through my big fat lie.

"Right." He rubs his hands together and looks at me excitedly. "Are you ready to make an honest man out of Rocco or do you want a getaway car? I'm cool with whatever."

I smile and shake my head at him. There really is just no way to stay mad at him. And I won't admit it out loud, but Sage and I may have possibly, just a teeny bit, deserved it. I guess it does get annoying that we try to parent them so often. Even if they act like teenagers most days.

I hug my dad around the middle but lean back enough to look up into his eyes and smile. "No getaway car needed. I am definitely marrying that man, no matter what."

Dad chuckles and shrugs. "Just had to make sure. It's my fatherly duty to offer you an escape if need be."

I grab his arm and tug. "Come on, let's get out there." I give him an evil grin. "Plus, I can't wait to see Sage's reaction when I tell her about the stunt you and Mom pulled in Vegas." I chirp before turning and walking towards the door.

"Now sweetheart, we can keep this just between us."

I look around the reception hall and can't believe that this is my life. I actually married the girl of my dreams today. The smile hasn't moved from my face since the moment that I saw Lav walking down the aisle towards me.

That's a sight that I'll remember until the day I die. I have never seen anything more beautiful than her in her gown. The smile that she had on her face was all for me. Neither one of us took our eyes off of each other until she reached my side.

Sitting here with my friends, celebrating my marriage, is an awesome feeling. I just don't know how I got so lucky. How a woman as magnificent as Lavender, chose me to be hers. I shake my head a little in disbelief.

"Why are you shaking your head like a dog that's just gotten wet?" Declan asks pulling me from my thoughts.

I smirk at the fool. "I was just wondering how I got so lucky to end up with Lavender." I say as I spot my bride across the room with some of her relatives.

I hear a bunch of scoffs from the rest of the guys sitting at the table with me. "Forcing yourself into her life probably has a great deal to do with it." JJ states with a smug grin.

Declan raises his beer bottle in the air. "Don't forget about knocking her up first. He wouldn't have had a leg to stand on if it wasn't for that."

Marc shakes his head. "No, it goes back to when he was pretty much pulling a Damon and showing up at the school all the time."

"My sister asked me to pick up my niece, what was I supposed to do?" I defend.

"I didn't realize that they let you have lunch with your kids. Good to know for when MJ gets to kindergarten." Morris says with a grin.

"That was only like once or twice." I mutter.

The all just stare blankly at me, damn traitors.

"It all worked out. Just leave him alone. He got the girl, end of story." Damon grunts out.

Declan looks over at his twin. "How many times are you going to use that damn line brother? Shit, it's like your fucking theme song these days."

We all laugh, well besides Damon, but that's just to be expected. "I like his take on it." I say.

JJ rolls his eyes and takes a sip of his beer. "Of course, you would. You two are practically cut from the same cloth at this point. The only thing you didn't do was try to kill her dumbass ex."

I unconsciously bare my teeth. I still hate thinking about that jackass. "No, but I definitely saw the appeal."

"Whatever happened with him anyway?" Morris questions while staring at Mellie's ass, as her and Shell dance to some annoying ass song.

"Last I heard, he got divorced, lost all custody of his kids and has pretty much become a full-time drunk. I still haven't figured out what he meant that night when he said that it was mine and Lavender's fault that his wife found out about his affair."

Damon and Declan give each other an odd glance that makes the hair on the back of my neck stand up. I'm not the only one who caught it either because JJ sighs loudly. "What did you two do now?" He asks defeatedly. Poor guy, it really must suck being in charge of us sometimes.

Declan looks at Damon and raises his eyebrow. "You need to tell him, since it was your idea."

This can't be good. Anything where Damon comes up with the idea can never be good. Marc perks right up at the sound of trouble. "You guys didn't call me?" He pouts, actually fucking pouts.

Damon gives him a glare. "No, because then the guy probably would've ended up getting hit by a car or driving off the edge of a cliff or some random shit like that."

Marc glares right back at him while leaning back in his seat. "Right, because him drink driving and T-boning Rocco's truck was so much better. Yeah, I can see exactly why you two should plan shit out."

I don't really want to admit it, but he kind of has a point. Judging by everyone else's expressions, they feel the same way.

"How the hell was I supposed to know that the dumb fuck would get shitfaced and then drive around town? I'm not a fucking psychic." Damon says while leaning forward and grasping onto the table.

"Calm down there *Hulk*, no need to get all worked up big guy." Declan drawls. "No one died, so it's fine. Just a weird turn of events, that's all. If anything, it's JJ's fault for jinxing everyone. That probably would've never happened if it wasn't for him."

JJ throws his arms up. "It was a damn slip of the tongue! It didn't count!"

I look over at Damon and raise my eyebrow in question. "What did you do?"

He starts fidgeting in his seat and looks like he's choosing his words carefully. "Once I found out how badly he treated Lavender, I decided to do some digging." He pauses and frowns at all of our blank looks. "I figured that I would find out something, so I watched him for a while."

"It's like a sickness with you isn't it? You can't even stop yourself from stalking people." Marc chuckles much to Damon's chagrin.

"Eh, in his defense, this wasn't so much stalking as following an idiot who made no attempt to hide his affair. Really, it was pretty blatant." Declan comes to his twin's defense.

"Okay, but why did you decide to do that in the first place? I mean, I appreciate man, but I just don't get it." I say.

Damon shrugs his massive shoulders. "None of us have had the best of luck when it comes to shit happening. Mel and Morris got kidnapped, Mel and Shell got held at gunpoint, Marc got shot and JJ's girls were held hostage by a crazy bitch with a knife. I figured that I should be proactive."

Okay, when he puts it like that, yeah it makes sense. We have had some shitty ass luck in the past few years. I guess he just has never seemed like the one to think about that.

I nod my head at him. "Okay, that's pretty sound. So, what did you end up finding out?"

He cracks his neck and looks at me with a smirk. "Well, when he cheated on Lavender he made sure that Lilly was extremely wealthy. Her trust fund alone would make most grown men weep. My guess is that he even knocked her up on purpose."

Morris frowns at him. "Why would you think that?"

Damon takes a sip of his beer before continuing. "Her parents are ultra conservative and religious. Having a baby out of wedlock is a big no-no for them. My guess, is that he knew it and used it to his advantage."

Marc scratches his chin and gives everyone a contemplative look. "I don't get why he would be so pissed off about it though. Shouldn't he be happy with a divorce? He gets to be free and gets a hefty pay day."

The rest of us nod our heads in agreement. That seems like the perfect scenario for him. Declan's snort has us all turning our heads towards him. He just shakes his head no. "Nope, this is his" – he points to Damon – "show, I was just along for the ride."

We all turn back to Damon like eager puppies begging for a treat. "That's where it gets interesting. Her daddy never liked Derrick and didn't trust him. So, he made that idiot sign a prenup that stated he would get nothing, not a single penny if he was caught cheating."

"So, he gets nothing?" I ask gleefully.

"Wouldn't they need to have proof during the court proceedings for the divorce?" JJ questions.

The smile that Damon gives us is best described as feral. "That's where my extra-curricular activities and the fact that my woman makes me take a million pictures of her and Jax came in handy." He says in a tone full of smugness. "All I did was make a house call, and it was just fate that her father happened to be there at the time, I handed over the pictures, gave him some information and went about the rest of my day."

I chuckle. "If that isn't poetic justice, I don't know what is. He cheated on Lavender to get rich and he lost it all while cheating again. Karma can be a bitch some days."

"Pretty much." Damon agrees.

I raise my bottle of beer into the air. "To Damon, the best stalker this world has ever seen."

The other guys raise theirs as well and help me toast the man who was able to get some form of justice for both Lavender and Lilly.

I shake my head. "Damn, I feel bad for Lilly though. Every time she looks at her kids, she's going to be reminded of him and everything he did for her money."

"Whose money?" Lavender asks, as she wraps her arms around my neck from behind.

I look up and smile at my beautiful bride. "Lilly, Damon was telling us everything that happened. I'll tell you about it later."

She takes a seat on my lap and puts her head on my shoulder. "No need. Michelle told us earlier. I feel bad for her too. Not only didn't she know that he was with me when they met, but then he does all of that to her."

She shifts around causing my dick to think that it's party time. Not yet buddy, but soon.

"I actually saw her in the grocery store last week." Lavender continues oblivious to my current problem. "We spoke for a few minutes. She's actually incredibly sweet and apologized over and over again. I just hope that one day she's able to find a decent man." Lav sighs.

"Hopefully one day." I say before kissing the side of her head.

JJ is tilting his head and I look at where he's looking and can't help but laugh.

"What?" Lavender asks.

I tilt my head to the left and she turns to look. She starts giggling uncontrollably.

"What is my wife doing?" JJ asks.

It takes a minute for Lav to get herself under control. "She's scolding our parents."

Declan leans forward excitedly while Kayla giggles from atop of Marc's lap. "Why? Did they try to have an orgie again?"

Lav snorts loudly. "No, that's the thing. They didn't want to in Vegas either. They were just mad that we kept treating them like children and decided to teach us a lesson."

"I don't get it." Morris says.

Lavenders lips twitch. "They realized how much they would embarrass Sage and I if they pulled a stunt like that. It was our punishment for getting rid of their *"herbal supplements"*, as my father likes to say."

JJ blinks at her a few times like he's not understanding any of what she just said. You can actually see the moment that he realizes it was all a joke. He gets at least three different shades of red, rapidly. "Are you fucking kidding me? My parents are still scared from that night. My mother has even said that she needs to be drunk the next time she's near your parents."

He gets up from the table swiftly and I grab onto his arm. "Where are you going?"

He looks down at me with a glare. "To help my wife scold her damn hippie parents."

He shrugs out of my grip and marches directly over to them, much to everyone else's amusement.

I give Lav a squeeze and thank God for tequila shots.

The End

Please consider leaving a review. Any and all feedback is appreciated. Even if you just leave a star rating. Every bit helps other readers find the book.

I love getting stalked by readers! Sign up for my Newsletter to stay up to date! Follow me on Facebook, Instagram, Twitter, Goodreads, and Bookbub!

Newsletter

Facebook

Instagram

Twitter

Goodreads

Bookbub

Website

About The Author

Nikki Mays is a pen name that was created from her maiden name. She is a wife and mother, who lives in a small town in New Jersey.

She has been with her husband for a decade and is surprised that he's still alive.

She began writing as a creative outlet after becoming a stay at home mom. She decided that she needed something exclusively for herself, not just being mommy.

She has two crazy boxers that love to keep that *"Evil"* mailman out of the yard. Besides writing and spending time with her little hellions, she enjoys cooking & baking.

Nikki loves to be stalked by her readers and encourages all interaction.